Hudson's Drove

Locomotion, in Darlington Railway Museum

Hudson's Drove

Bruce Robinson

Elmstead Publications
Wicklewood, Norfolk, NR18 9QL
Published 2000

© Bruce Robinson

Elmstead Publications
Elmstead, Milestone Lane, Wicklewood
Norfolk, NR18 9QL

First published 2000

ISBN: 0 9523379 75

British Library Cataloguing in Publication Data. A catalogue
record for this book is available from the British Library

Text input and book design by the author using a DTP system
with PageMaker 6.5. Main text font: Palatino

Printed by Geo Reeve, Ltd, Wymondham, Norfolk

Photographs and map by the author

Acknowledgements

THIS novel grew from a desire to write something about an earlier generation faced by far-reaching change, and about that immensely resilient breed, the long-distance cattle drover. Very largely bypassed by popular histories and the literary world, they nevertheless made a critical and significant contribution to the commercial life and fabric of the countryside for many generations. In the end my research involved a great deal of reading and a fascinating 350-mile journey retracing the steps of the drovers from the Lowther Hills, north of Dumfries, all the way back to Norfolk.

It is necessary to point out that although many of the locations and places mentioned in the text are genuine, most of the characters and the entire story are fiction. It is also necessary to say that, inevitably, I owe a huge debt of gratitude to the work of a multitude of writers who have already tackled aspects of the two periods in question which are, roughly, 1829 and 1880. Naturally I have tried to make the flavour, the detail and the words as authentic as possible, but I sense an opportunity for historians to pick holes in it. All I can say is that the errors and omissions are entirely my own work. That said, I acknowledge the particular usefulness of certain specific sources, and happily list them below.

For Blakeney and the railway question I went to The Glaven Ports (Jonathan Hooton, Blakeney History Group, 1996), while Classic Landforms of the North Norfolk Coast (EM Bridges, The Geographical Association, 1998) supplied geological information. Then again, Bryant's Map of Norfolk in 1826 (The Larks Press, 1998), the Ordnance Survey map of Norfolk, 1887 (sheet 38, Cromer; David & Charles reprint, 1982), and the Ordnance Survey Pathfinder map No 745 (East Retford and Blyth, 1987), all offered topographical cues.

Cooper Henderson and the Open Road (Charles Lane, Allen & Co, 1984) described some of the many types of road carriage in picture and text form; impressions of the original Stockton and Darlington railway came from The Darlington Railway Centre & Museum (which also houses Stephenson's Locomotion engine) and The Guardian newspaper, September 11 and November 14, 1998; while some detail was gleaned from a print of the watercolour painting Opening of the Stockton & Darlington Railway, 1825, by John Dobbin (1815-1888). A History of Long Sutton & District (FW & BA Robinson, Long Sutton Civic Society, reprint, 1995) described the construction of the Sutton Wash crossing; and A History of County Durham (D Pocock & R Norris, Phillimore, 1990) added period detail.

General information about the 19th century was also found in The Batsford Companion to Local History (Stephen Friar, Batsford, 1991); White's 1845 Norfolk (David & Charles Reprints, 1969); the Chronology of World History: The Modern World, 1763-1992 (Neville Williams & Philip Waller, Helicon, 2nd edition, 1995); the Rev. BJ Armstrong's A Norfolk Diary, 1850-1887 (Harrap, 1949); Geography of the County of Norfolk, by the Rev. D Morris (1870s; facsimile edition, David Wright, 1995); Emigration from East Anglia in the 1830s (Robert Malster, article, The Annual, bulletin of the Norfolk Archaeological & Historical Research Group, No 7, 1998) and The Book of Household Management (Mrs Isabella Beeton, Ward, Lock & Bowden, 1895).

Descriptions of inns during the coaching age came from The Book of the Inn (edited Thomas Burke, Constable, 1927), and The Old Inns of England (AE Richardson, Batsford, 1934); with other 19th century details from The Old North Road through Babworth Parish (Joan Board, Happy Walking, 1998); The First Man to Walk Hadrian's Wall, 1802 (William Hutton, Frank Graham reprint, 1990); Dumfries 200 Years Ago (Rev William Burnside, Fine Lines Publishing, 1998); and Living in Old Retford (BJ Biggs, Eaton Hall College, 1973).

Information on Warham Camp came from The Iron Age Forts of Norfolk (East Anglian Archaeology, EAA 54, 1991), and a description of the Peterloo Massacre from The Guardian (May 8, 1996), and other places. The telephone episode was fashioned from information in The First 100 Years of Telephones Viewed from Norwich (Eric Clayton, British Telecom, 1980), and from Mr Armstrong's diary; while the Eastern Daily Press (November 9, 1998) gave details of a public debate on the Flat Earth theory in 1871. Not unnaturally, the flavour of Julius Caesar's evidently disputed crossing of the Channel was culled from the original source, Julius Caesar: Did He Cross the Channel? (Scott Surtees, John Smith, 1866).

Background about Holt and the church of St Andrew the Apostle was garnered from Holt: Historic Georgian Town (Town Guide, Chamber of Commerce), Holt Town Walks (The Holt Society), and The Story of Holt (Jean Smith & John Pocock); while On The Parish: Recorded Lives of the Poor of Holt and District 1780-1835 (Jane Hales, The Larks Press, 1994) reprinted a graphic selection of local settlement hearings.

As for drovers and droving, the most satisfying sources were: St Faith's Fair (Julian Eve, articles, The Quarterly, Norfolk Archaeological & Historical Research Group, Nos 6 & 7, 1992); Shirley Toulson's The Drovers (Shire Publications, 1980); WH Murray's Rob Roy MacGregor (Canongate, 1995); KJ Bonser's indispensable The Drovers (County Book Club, 1972); and The

Drove Roads of Scotland (Nelson, 1960) and New Ways Through the Glens (House of Lochar edition, 1995), both by the admirable ARB Haldane.

Finally, my thanks to the Bassetlaw Museum, East Retford (for advice and information); to Dumfries Local History Museum; and last but not least to Cynthia, for helping me through the difficult bits.

Once again, the reader should bear in mind that despite the use of real settings, and in some cases real names, this is a work of fiction and that no actual representation of any person, living or dead, is intended.

By the same author

A History of Long Sutton (South Lincolnshire) Produced privately 1965 (with FW Robinson)

The Peddars Way The Weathercock Press 1978

A Skylark Descending (Novel) Robert Hale, 1978

History of Long Sutton & District Long Sutton Civil Trust 1981 (with FW Robinson), reprinted 1995

Norfolk Origins 1: Hunters to First Farmers Acorn Editions 1981 (with Andrew Lawson)

Norfolk Origins 2: Roads & Tracks Poppyland Publishing 1983 (with Edwin Rose)

The Peddars Way & Norfolk Coast Path Countryside Commission 1986

Norfolk Origins 3: Celtic Fire & Roman Rule Poppyland Publishing 1987 (with Tony Gregory)

Peddars Way & Norfolk Coast Path Aurum Press 1992, reprinted 1996

Norfolk Fragments Elmstead Publications 1994

A Glimpse of Distant Hills (Novel) Elmstead Publications 1995

Chasing the Shadows: Norfolk Mysteries Revisited Elmstead Publications 1996

Passing Seasons: a watching brief on 50 years of football Elmstead Publications 1997

The Norfolk Walker's Book Elmstead Publications 1998

Some explanations

abolitionists - anti-slavery movement supporters
ague - a kind of malarial fever
antics - clowns

badger - licensed corn carrier
bagman - commercial traveller on horseback carrying samples in saddlebags
bannock - round, flat, unsweetened oatmeal or barley cake baked on griddle, still sold in Dumfries
bar - site of toll bar
barouche - four-wheeled horse-drawn carriage
beck - brook
Bill of Exchange/Promissory Note - a promise to pay; system of credit; bills handed around (as banknotes)
blackmail - mail (in the old sense) meant tax, rent or tribute; protection money; payment exorted by intimidation
Board of Ordnance - forerunner of Ordnance Survey
Boots - handyman at inn; carried luggage, cleaned footwear, etc
brogger - itinerant; one who traded in small quantities (often wool)
brose - pease porridge, sometimes with butter/fat added; Atholl brose a mixture of whisky and honey left to ferment
bosky - wooded
Bullock Hill - site of annual St Faith's Fair, near Norwich
bush house - private house brewing or selling beer, advertised by bush or greenery hanging outside

carstone - dark brown sandstone, as exposed in cliffs at Hunstanton
causey - causeway; sometimes called a ramper
Cetywayo - King of Zululand; captured after annexation of Transvaal in 1877 and brought to England
chaise - see post-chaise
chariot - private carriage drawn by two or four horses with postillians riding nearside horses, footman at rear; forward-facing seat for two; luggage on top and rear

chaldrons - (Durham) horse-drawn waggons (mid-17th century) running on planks or waggon-ways; later with flanged/cast iron wheels

clove - divided hoof of the cow

cob - thickset draught and riding horse

coggles - pebbles

cottar - cottager

cowpox - produced raised pustules on dairymaids' hands; believed to protect from smallpox

crewe yard - bedded or strawed yard, enclosure for wintering cattle

crowdie - cold water oatmeal porridge

cue/s (sometimes kew/s) - crescent-shaped iron shoe/s for cattle

diligence - four-wheeled conveyance, often heavily laden, sometimes drawn by six horses

dried neat - dried beef

drift (of cattle), driftway - herd; cattle road

driver - drovers' assistant who helped control herds; sometimes on foot, sometimes mounted

drove - cattle road to field or summer grazing; cattle being driven

Fay's Fair - Norfolk cattle fair; after St Faith's feast day, latterly October 17

fleak - wattled hurdle

fodder - roots, hay or straw fed to livestock

gate - road or way, opening or entrance

halt (sometimes holt) - cattle rest place (also paddle)

higgler - dealer in poultry and eggs

holt - small plantation of trees

hosen - leggings

Isandhlwana - scene of battle in 1879 between Zulus and British troops; British losses topped 800

jagger - man in charge of packhorse train, mainly North Country (see train master)

kidder - goat herder

kyloes - tawny, small-bodied cattle from Isle of Skye

Macadam - John Loudon Macadam (born 1756), Scottish engineer, who with Telford and others did much to improve quality of road surfaces

manner - manure (see tad)

murrain - generic name for cattle plague, anthrax, foot & mouth (see rinderpest)

neat - cattle retaining horns (see polled**)**

oatmeal - served as porridge, bannock, brose or Atholl brose; oaten bread was oatmeal mixed with water

opium poppy - often grown in cottage gardens; poppy 'tea' and laudenum used to combat many ailments

ostler - stableman, usually at inn

pad - footpath

paddle - grazing ground for cattle (also halt)

pike, pikeman - turnpike, turnpike gatekeeper

pinfold - parish animal pound

polled - cattle with horns removed, also called hough (see neat)

post-chaise - vehicle for hire, often at inns

Puseyism - after Edward Pusey (1800-1882), British divine, who laid down principles on which High Church movement was founded

raiks - stone walls beside drove roads to stop cattle "streaming" over private land

ramper - raised road (causeway) to protect from flooding

reiving/reivers - cattle stealing particularly in Scotland (circa 1740); double dealing

riggling - haggling, bargaining

rinderpest - acute contagious viral disease of cattle; also called distemper (see murrain)

runnel - small stream or groove

Sassenach - English person, or sometimes Lowland Scot

Scots' runts - black Scottish cattle

seethe (pots, on fire) - simmer, boil

settlement - from 1795 and before Poor Law Amendment Act of 1834, people could not be removed from a parish until they actually became a chargeable liability, then they had to obtain a certificate of settlement, which required examination under oath by two local magistrates

shock - sheaf of corn, stacked in tens for tithe purposes

shutter stations - line of shutter signal towers (1806 - 1814) from The Admiralty (London) to Yarmouth, through Barnham, East Harling, Carleton Rode, Wreningham, Thorpe, Strumpshaw

skid - braking lever device to control coaches down hill, operated by rear coachman with rope

Siemens - electrical engineering firm

smelteries - (Durham) plants for processing ore

smiddy - smithy

sprit - sapling

stance (eg, stanced; or halt) - overnight grazing/rest area for cattle (word still used in Dumfries, ie bus stance, taxi stance)

stance money - grazing rent

stirks - half grown cattle

tad - manure (see manner)

talbot - packhorse master's favourite dog

tenters/tenter-boys - lads employed to keep birds from corn and cattle from straying

tessera - the building blocks of mosiacs

tilt - canvas awning over carrier's waggon

topsman - rode ahead of herd to arrange route and grazing

train - line of packhorses, sometimes up to 40, often Galloway ponies

train master - man in charge of packhorse train (see jagger)

trousing - breeches with stocking

truck - barter

tryst - gathering place, cattle fair (mainly Scotland**)**

United Telephone Company - formed 1880 from earlier Bell and Edison concerns

wathe/warth/wath - ford

Whip - lead driver (most often of coach, or possibly waggon)

whiskey - small cart

Wolseley, Garnet - British officer of the Burma, Crimea, India and China campaigns; key figure in Zulu War; captured Cetywayo; remembered in Norwich by Market Place pub name

yan, teyan, tethera - Scotch drovers' method of counting; one version continued: lethera, dic, sezar, laizar, catra, horna, tic (10); yan-a-tic (11), teyan-a-tic (12), tethera-a-tic (13), etc; mether-a-tic, bub-yan-a-bub, teyan-a-bub, mether-a-bub, etc; gigget (20); there were many local variations

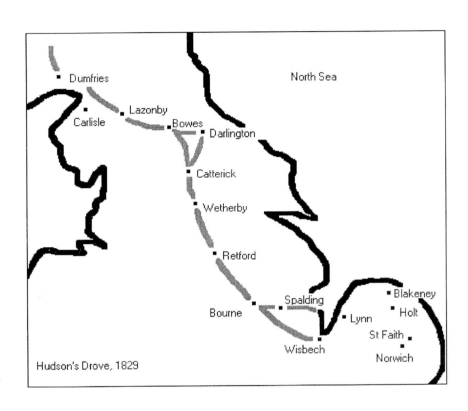

North Sea

Dumfries

Lazonby
Carlisle
Bowes
Darlington

Catterick

Wetherby

Retford

Spalding
Blakeney
Bourne
Holt
Lynn
St Faith
Wisbech
Norwich

Hudson's Drove, 1829

A Sort of Prologue

Norwich, Norfolk
January, 2000

WE ALL search, I suppose, some for the elusive pot of gold, some for enlightenment. The range is wide, the objectives too numerous to calculate. Unnumberable, even. In my own case it is usually books, especially second hand books. There is no particular reason for this aberration save that new books are often expensive and there is a vicarious sort of pleasure to be gained from hunting down and finally cornering a bargain. You see, I particularly enjoy the search, the hunt, the musty atmosphere of most of the mouldering shops. And I certainly relish the ping of delight as among tomes buried deep on some barely remembered and slumbering, undisturbed shelf there is revealed, completely unexpectedly, a long sought and yearned-for title, some long forgotten treasure which I can now return to the sunlight. And even then there are more pleasures to come. Handle the book and feel the covers, polished to a sheen by countless, unknown others; open the covers and smell the paper, rich and mature like good wine; see the finger marks and turning-downs and sometimes even the jottings of earlier owners who have loved or loathed it, but whom the book will have moved or influenced, for better or for worse. For example, I once found, in an "anything for one pound" box, a volume called "The Village Labourer, 1760-1832: a Study in the Government of England before the Reform Bill." On an inside leaf was inscribed, in a careful hand, "Presented to," and then the name of a reverend gentleman, "as a token of esteem and in memory of happy times spent together at the New Cross fireside. 1930-1931." I have often tried to imagine those two friends, smoking and talking, relaxing and remembering, warming their toes before the fire, perhaps enjoying a convivial pint. And yes, the book itself was informative. But I plead guilty to having enjoyed the inscription more than the text. Even so, I would not part with it for the worlds. The fading echo of those two friends is safe with me; for a little longer, that is.

My own subjects are walking (did you know it had a history?) and, mainly but not always, local history, and then again only specific subjects. Travel and descriptions, the Iron Age and the Romans and the roads and tracks they left behind. Thus I tend to haunt specific shelves. UK History. English History. East Anglia. Roman Britain. Prehistory. Transport and Communications. Walking. And sometimes even Fiction, for I am also partial to Dickens and Hemingway, Hardy and HE Bates. Cunning bookshop owners have thought of a myriad of labels behind which to conceal and guard their treasures, but sometimes I have the best of the contest. A month ago, in a box of discards in the corner of an otherwise empty second hand bookshop, I rummaged around and found a rather nice 1909 edition (Chatto & Windus, actually) of Robert Louis Stevenson's Essays of Travel, well thumbed but in perfect condition and plainly once much loved. Now it is being loved again. Meanwhile, and having just finished reading Celia Fiennes, I am now searching for DeQuincey's walks in Wales.

But all that is largely by the by. I was about to tell you of my last expedition but one, inspired by the passing comment of a likewise interested acquaintance that Holt was worth looking at, particularly a little second hand bookshop he had discovered and spent some time in, spotting among other things Harper's The Norwich Road, 1901, and an evidently tattered 1913 copy of Sidney and Beatrice Webb's The Story of the King's Highway. He thought there might be others to interest me. And so a few days later I finally disentangled myself from the headlong rush of commuter traffic on the city ring road, escaped into a slowly increasing amount of road space along by the city airport, and made my way to that market town which, to my shame, I seem to have generally but quite unconsciously neglected in my travels. Thankfully, Holt was forgiving. It welcomed me with frosty, sharp sunshine, and even left a parking space for my convenience.

I think it was Hilaire Belloc (a compulsive walker, by the way) who said there were only two certainties about a journey, the beginning and the end. Perhaps it was typical of him to have ignored the reality of the between-times, for it was evidently his forte to visit his wife, impregnate her and then, under the guise either of a man of letters seeking inspiration or of a tourist loaded with religiosity, he would be off on some jaunt or other so that they would endure their gestation periods apart, in different places. My own between-times was equally productive, however, for having been given fairly precise directions by my acquaintance I strolled through the busy town and found the old bookshop within ten minutes, and without difficulty.

It was in a side street, as so many of them are, and if there was a word to describe my immediate reaction it would be, I suppose, inauspicious. The shop sat there quietly, out of the limelight, silent to matters of advertising and self promotion, modest, mutely accepting its lowly station in the commercial life of the town; private, almost. The paintwork, once dark green and now mottled by the seasons, looked like lichen advancing over a dying trunk, and even the single window (windows always give bookshop problems, because sunlight destroys the goods) was a patchwork of pieces of grimy card, designed to increase the shade, behind which it was nevertheless possible to glimpse the spines and occasional covers of cascades of books which were once in orderly rows and piles but had subsequently been disturbed and poked and prodded and had not been re-sorted. I grasped the door handle, a gnarled knob of a thing, heard the dull tinkle of the inevitable bell, and stepped into the gloom.

With churches - Anglican churches, anyway - the moment you step inside you are assailed by a smell which I can only describe as a subtle mixture of furniture polish, mothballs and antiquity. Here in the gloom in Holt was the scent of the archetypal second hand bookshop, a nasal cornucopia of dust tinged with a touch of crumbling wall plaster and damp, antique shelves, piled books and stale air, coupled with a tiny frisson of stale tobacco smoke evidently left behind by the last customer but one who spent ten minutes running his hands and eyes along the poetry shelves, pipe clenched in mouth, and then left without buying anything. It was the smell of words, long ignored, crumbling to nothing. The old walls were white-washed, from what one could see between the shelves, and the lighting was from bare, unadorned bulbs. One tiny room led into another, so that one moved into the honeycomb without knowing where you were going and with one's line of vision abruptly blocked in all directions by mountainsides of books and tall timber shelves. In one room, as I blinked and tried to adjust to the light, just beyond Philosophy and to the left of Architecture, I glimpsed the elderly keeper, presumably the owner, a short, shrivelled, bent man in shirt sleeves and waistcoat, sitting on a stool beside a desk laden with papers and books and notes, pencils and Biros, jars of elastic bands and dishes of paper clips, a tangle of stamps and stamp pads, piles of accounts and scribbled notes and all the untidy paraphenalia of ancient commerce. To his right, on the edge of the desk, was an equally elderly cash till. He appeared to be studying a newspaper, and he did not look up as I went by.

The shelves I sought were, inevitably, at the furthest end of the honeycomb, in the last room, and for twenty minutes, lost to the world, I rummaged through General History and British Palaeolithic, and then Norfolk/East Anglian Interest, with a growing feeling that I was entombed somewhere deep beneath the surface of the earth. There was little to interest me save some Jane Hales, which I already had, and a rather dilapidated copy of Lucilla Reeve's Breckland tale The Earth No Longer Bare, written in 1939. My own copy was in better shape. I was not tempted, and moved to turn away, and it was then I realised the bent little man was standing a stride or two from my right shoulder, regarding me intently, and that I did not know how long he had been there.

"History?" he asked sharply.

"Local history, actually," I replied, whereupon he muttered something I did not catch and then wandered away, leaving me to the silence of the tomb. Ten minutes later, having completed a circuit of Archaeology and even Dramatic Criticism, and in trying to retrace my steps back to the exit, I happened to pass through the tiny, cramped room in which he had his desk, his stool and his cash till, and this time he watched he quietly and intently, like an eagle, as I passed.

"Nothing?" he said suddenly.

"No. Actually, I was looking for DeQuincey."

"I've no DeQuincey," he replied with startling certainly, as though he knew every book in the shop. "Scarce. But he's not read nowadays."

"Or local history, but I seem to have got most of them. I like the rare stuff, really."

The little man thought for a moment and then unfolded himself from his stool and wordlessly beckoned to me to follow him. We worked our way past World/General, through the two rooms of Fiction, and finally came to Poetry. This was new country to me, and yet behind these shelves was yet another bulging shelf. The label said Diaries/Journals. He paused for a moment, ran his bright eyes over the jumbled spines, and finally withdrew what looked like a small Morocco-covered notebook. He gave it to me to peruse.

"TW Hume, " he said. "Personal journal, though he calls it a commonplace book, which may be an error. Impressions of Holt, mid-19th century. Hand written, a nice piece of Victoriana. Acquired it last year."

"I've never heard of TW Hume."

"A minor Holt antiquarian. Wrote several essays on local history, I believe. I can find out more about him if you want."

In the end I did not purchase the journal, not there and then. I did spend some time looking through it, and found the references to droving interesting, and discussed with him a price, which seemed unusually high, and finally decided I needed time to think about it. If the journal had been on his shelves unsold since last year then it was hardly in great demand, I reasoned. Eventually I said maybe, but not now, so he replaced it carefully back on the shelf and I drove back to Norwich wondering if I had missed something. At home, bemoaning a lack of success in my search for the DeQuincey, I discovered that almost as uppermost in my mind was a growing realisiation that I did, after all, want the Hume journal. It was calling me. Anyway, three days' later I re-traced my steps to Holt, parked the car, this time with difficulty and only after two circuits of the town, walked back to the bookshop and once again heard the tired tinkle of the door bell. The owner was still there, still seated on his stool, still alone.

"The Hume journal. Do you still have it?"

"Yes."

"I've changed my mind."

"I thought you might. I'll fetch it for you."

Moments later the journal was back in my hands, where it was destined to be, and I paid for it, quickly. The till clanked and clattered, and he handed me my change and with it another piece of paper.

"I did some research. Thought you might like to have the additional details," he said.

The note was typewritten and headed: "TW Hume of Holt." It continued: "Thomas Westcott Hume's father owned a paper-making and printing business in Huntingdon; his mother, Florence Westcott, was from a moderately well-to-do Huntingdon family. Thomas was born there in 1813, an only child. As a youth he was sent to Holt to attend Gresham's School, then based in the Market Place, and never seems to have returned to the family home or to the family business. He was evidently comfortably off, thanks to an income from the business, and seems to have liked Norfolk and enjoyed the social life, developing particular interests in archaeology and local history. In later life he compiled several essays on aspects of local history, wrote and published several pamphlets, and acquired a considerable library of Holt and Norfolk material. Married Charlotte Sophia Webb, a local family. They seem to have lived a quiet life in a house in Bull Street, off Fish Hill, where he was able to pursue his particular interests. Died 1884, aged 71, of some winter ailment or other; buried Holt churchyard. Charlotte survived him until 1892, dying when she was 74. There were no children. Later that same year, 1892, the house in Bull Street was sold, along with the contents, which were dispersed."

I folded the paper and placed it inside the pages of the journal for safe keeping.

"Did you find that information on the internet?" I asked, somewhat mischeviously.

He looked at me, puzzled, and then annoyed.

"No, I did not. I researched it, looking up the directories and other appropriate sources."

For some reason I pursued the subject.

"Do you have a computer in the shop?"

"No, I do not."

"No web site or internet, then? I thought no book shop could survive without one nowadays."

"I shall not have an internet or a computer. And you are quite right, I shall not survive. I do not love internets. I love books."

Later on, back in Norwich, it occurred to me I had been unusually rude to the poor man whose own shop and stock would one day probably be sold and dispersed. It would be one less potential source of treasure, one less mausoleum of crumbling words, one less thread connecting with the past. However, safe on my shelves I now have Hume's journal and the book dealer's typewritten note, and sometimes I sit down with them for a browse. Temporarily, the Hume writings and the journal are safe with me. Until the time of my own dispersal, of course.

Mr Hume's Reminiscences

Holt, Norfolk
Friday, January 8, 1880

I RECALL the Shire Hall hearing with great clarity for a number of reasons, only one of which was the tenor of my own life in those days, meaning my thoroughly unwholesome and unappetising immaturity, and a sense, foolishly conceived I am sure, of being at the centre of things. In truth, my paltry score that season was but twenty callow summers. It still grieves me that youth is so persistently consumed by droll thoughts and feelings. My father most certainly warned and counselled against them, and of the consequences of my folly if I did not desist, perhaps recognising in me precisely the same inclination to wild demeanour and irresponsible behaviour which blighted the early years of his own dissolute bachelor years. As it turned out his subsequent marriage was the salvation of him, as I dare say mine was for me, yet I readily confess to having been born in the image of him, for I became a considerable parental trial and worry, as he was to his.

There was, therefore, a naive and unfortunate importance attached to the Shire Hall proceedings, particularly among the young, a sense of excitement ennobled by the interest of not only myself and my louche companions of the time, but by much of Holt and its nearest neighbourhood. Another strand contributing to the clarity of my recollection was my father's distaste for the entire business, and his insistence, when we discussed the matter, that Hudson must have been the creator of his own problems and that the law should be left to follow its majestic and inevitable course. The whiff of local scandal was therefore as strong as the stench of powder following the discharge of a fowling piece, and it drew a crowd of curious, chattering onlookers. Yet another strand was that I knew Hudson slightly, by acquaintance of course, for he was by then, in 1833, a dispossessed labourer of exceeding low circumstance, a cause of some sadness to many people - other than to my father - for Hudson had been, despite his troubles and difficulties, a man of considerable reputation, mainly, and strangely as it turned out, for his integrity and honesty.

Yet there we all were on the appointed day, ignoring the chill, congregated in the Plain around the front door of the Shire Hall, awaiting the completion of business and the adjudication of the Justices, placing wagers for trifling sums on the outcome and generally surrounding the whole episode with a veneer of light headed frivolity. I dare say after it was all over we repaired at speed to The Feathers, which was our usual wont - though some preferred the Queen Adelaide in Withers Street - but I cannot say this was so with hand on heart because in some areas my memory, nearly fifty years after the event, has diminished.

What I can say with certainty is that a rash of anticipation quite suddenly rippled among the crowd when it was realised the Justices had delivered their verdict and that Hudson, in consequence, was on his way out. The crowd milled about the door, talking and jostling, and I, standing beside the wall of the Shire Hall, and perceiving an opportunity, clambered on to the mounting block to enhance my view and was thus able to witness most of the admittedly brief proceedings over the heads of the rest of the throng.

There was a hum of renewed anticipation as Hudson himself emerged from the gloom of the interior on to the step. He was unaccompanied, seemingly unaffected, bare headed, and dressed in a very poor way indeed. For one moment a look of alarm flickered across his eyes when he caught sight of the crowd for the first time. Then he paused, evidently quite calm and otherwise expressionless, glanced upwards at the clear, cold sky, drew his clothing around him and stepped forward, boldly I would say, and disappeared into the midst of a confused mass of bodies. Then, seconds later, a quite curious thing occurred. With the crowd milling around, anxious to be appraised of the verdict and to witness the disgrace of this hitherto good man, a small neutral space appeared around Hudson so that, for a moment, I could see him again, and into that space there stepped an urchin carrying a small wallet, or bag, who spoke to him. Hudson stooped momentarily to hear the words above the hubbub, received the bag from the urchin, examined it with a puzzled expression, pocketed it, and then walked on.

Of course, everyone shouted questions at once, but no one actually gleaned any additional information. Nevertheless, it was a very particular, crystalline moment, for in the months following I saw Hudson only once more, and then fleetingly, exchanging merely a tacit nod of recognition. Not that our paths would normally have crossed, you understand, except in the way of business of which, at this stage, he had none. He was a broken man.

I recollect now that the hearing was in September, 1833, and he, poor fellow, survived a mere five or six years further. To the best of my knowledge no one ever took the trouble to erect a memorial to mark his final resting place. Perhaps he was considered in some way unworthy, or more likely, perhaps, no one wanted the stigma of being in some way attached to him, however minor the association. It was gross calumny.

Fallen from his high estate,
And welt'ring in his blood:
Deserted at his utmost need
By those his former bounty fed;
On the bare earth expos'd he lies,
With not a friend to close his eyes.
(John Dryden, 1631-1700, Alexander's Feast)
Just so.

A break in concentration. A minor altercation at the front door. There was the tinkle of the outdoor bell, then an urgent knocking, followed by Emily's footfalls hurrying down the hall and the low murmur of voices. Without the recourse of peering from my window I knew immediately who it was. William Harcourt, a tidy and respectable smallholder with acres on the far side of Great Wood towards Kelling who, knowing my expertise and reputation in matters archaeological, had brought for my consideration and identification another package of fragments gleaned from his fields. This has occurred before. Indeed, he has turned up at my front door so many times and with so many pieces of pottery and coins and glass that Emily now has a routine to deal with the matter. She will not admit him, explaining that I am engaged on urgent business - which in all honesty may be nothing more onerous than scribbling at my desk, musing on the view from the window or sitting before the fire perusing the pages of the Norwich Eastern Daily Press - though she will receive the package. Then she will take it to the scullery and in due course wash the fragments in a bucket of water, and the next day, when they are dry, place them for inspection on my desk in the study when she comes in to tidy and to lay the fire. Later, I will drop him a note thanking him for his consideration, describing what he has found.

Harcourt is a decent enough fellow, but it is a trifling matter, a minor distraction save for one thought. I have learned from others that Harcourt now wanders the fields quite distractedly looking for fragments in the furrows and among the clods and he is, I confess, more proficient than I shall ever be in finding pieces. Inevitably, most of them will be from an area north of the town that, judging by the frequency and value of his discoveries, seems to have attracted the Roman person to such an extent I am beginning to suspect the presence of a settlement in that vicinity. On the other hand, perhaps a lack of inquiring Harcourts in other areas has given his acres an overstated importance. We shall see. On my next visit to Norwich I shall attend the library of the Archaeological Society, if I can learn to abide the inbred irascibility and smoking habits of most of the elders who appear to reside there, to study such records as may be available.

Thursday the 14th

All this, however, was a digression, and having recently re-read all that I had written earlier I fear there is now a need to regress and explain the matter before me in greater detail. Christmas was a delight, made even more so by my dear wife's ability to so delicately decorate each and every room and imbue the entire house with what I can only describe as welcomeness. I complimented her on the matter, several times. Everywhere there was warmth and colour, joy and, happy to relate, abstemious piety.

On Christmas Eve and again on Christmas Day itself we attended service at St Andrew's, during which Mr Brumell preached rather well indeed, I thought, on the subject of the war and the Christmas message, and the need for faith; and during the afternoon, the threatened snow having resisted an urge to cushion everything in a blanket of white silence, my dear wife and I ordered out the pony and cart and engaged the ostler's boy from the Angel in Bull Street to take us through the crispness and pale sunshine to Fishmongers' Wood and then along Norwich Road to the common where we strolled for a time acknowledging many of our dear friends, exchanging the felicitations of the season. The next day being Boxing Day we entertained. Then with the guests having gone and the tidying ended we agreed that Emily, whom I rewarded with a few extra coins, should take time to visit her family in Thornage. I offered to pay for the ostler's lad to take her, but she said she did not like him, and preferred to walk, though my dear wife heard later that Emily's brother had fetched her.

Having no children to entertain, or to entertain us, it has been our habit to divide our Christmas festivities into three, our own Yuletide triptych, namely, Church, Friends, Conviviality, and further, to present each other with small trifles, or presents, during the early evening of Christmas Day. This is precisely what happened immediately on the return from our outing when we were still aglow with the cold air and the exhilaration of the ride, and flushed by the welcome warmth of the fire. I gave my dear wife a rather pretty wrist bracelet, inset with amber stones, which I had admired and acquired in Norwich on the occasion of my last visit, and she gave me this commonplace book for my thoughts and jottings. I believe commonplace book to be an appropriate title, for it is not a diary and I shall not keep it as a journal, both these tasks demanding regular and diligent attendance, something I do not feel is within my character. So commonplace book it is. In the event it is also, I have to confess, a rather fine production of morocco goatskin leather binding, marbled end papers and a good quality of page therein. Moreover, it begs to be written in. At least, it handles rather well, opens with a satisfying crispness, sits flat on my desk, and presents to my pen a surface that feels and sounds very pleasant indeed. In the meantime, I have decided I shall make only occasional entries, of things that interest me. Nor shall I enter every date, for I have never been fond of boundaries and categories that seem to achieve little more than the restriction of intellectual preoccupation.

Later
The Pembertons visited, quite with prior notice or prior preparation, but it was a pleasant moment despite Emily being off duty and my dear wife having to cope with all the hospitalities. Opened a bottle of Lochnagar scotch whisky, which I believe has been praised by our Queen, and Pemberton and I proclaimed it passably good, though a trifle dry for my palate.
   A little snow this evening, and a pleasing quietness abroad in the streets.

January the 17th
Spoke to my dear wife during breakfast on my recent recollection of poor drover Hudson and the hearing, and matters of similar recall, and she reminded me that Hudson's journal still resides somewhere in our roof among the trunks and boxes, dust, and spare furniture. Also, in my study I have a copy of the Justices' evidence and finding at Hudson's hearing, culled from the records many years ago. I must rediscover it one day; and have resolved to send Emily up the ladder into the roof to recover the journal. It is many years since I saw it. For the life of me I cannot now recollect much of what happened to Hudson after the hearing, but I do recall wondering belatedly if the process of Law had not treated him somewhat shabbily, and with undue harshness.

February, morning
A distressing month, grey and unprepossessing, consistent cold and damp, and equally depressing news of the War, which has gone uniformly badly since Isandhlwana despite Garnet Wolseley's pursuit of Cetywayo. At least the study fire is piled high and light from the flame flickers across the ceiling. Soon I shall have to light the lamp, too, for such is the gloom it will shortly be too dark to write without the assistance of an additional flame near my desk. It reminds me of an item in a recent newspaper to the effect that electricity may soon have the streets of New York awash with light,

thanks to Siemens, apparently before the year is out. Well, that may be so. America is renowned for its forwardness in many things, and despite the fact we British are ever open to all new ideas and useful inventions, even to the extraordinary extent that meat brought all the way from Australia apparently in a frozen state can now be bought in London, I do not think motive power or lighting by electricity will do for us. Our steam railway system is the envy of the world beyond the Empire, and our town soon to join it, and here in Holt our glowing gas lamps serve us nobly. Indeed, our streets after nightfall are utterly safe, for near-do-wells are repelled by bright light as moths are attracted to it.

Later, after noon
My desk is at the window over our front door in Bull Street, overlooking Fish Hill, so that I may sit and work and observe people about their business, though in truth few give much impression of having business to do. It is still damp and cold and there is a noticeable amount of aimless wandering, strolling and gossiping. At irregular intervals a horse clatters by; or a delivery boy, hunched against the chill, scuttles across the plain carrying a parcel or a sack; or a well-wrapped family pauses and gazes into a shop window. It is strangely satisfying to watch them, for it makes me think of my own small family, warm and snug inside. Now a murmur of voices reaches me from downstairs, and sometimes a polite gust of restrained laughter, which is my dear wife entertaining visiting acquaintances in the sitting-room. Cook is in the kitchen and Emily in her room above my study, having seen to the ladies in the sitting-room and now resting before she begins to clear away and then help cook prepare dinner, and the ostler's lad is in the yard cleaning the cart harness. I can hear buckets clattering and the occasional cheerful call, his voice echoing in the passageway as he sees someone he recognises pass across the plain. It is all remarkably humble and homely, and I do think that if I were in some foreign land, and inclined to think of England, this is the scene and these are the sounds that would come to me.

Still February
There is to be a British election next month which, we can but pray, may go some way to answering the Irish question. Meanwhile, the news from the War is still decidedly distressing.

April the second
This is an entry I have been contemplating for some time as I may have introduced a sense of confusion into my writing, and now wish to put the matter satisfactorily to right. Some time ago I described Hudson as a pen-

niless and dispossessed labourer in lowly circumstance, which in 1833 he plainly and truthfully was, and went on to say he left a journal, written, if memory serves me correctly, in 1829, which infers that pens and writing were by no means strangers to him. Some may see this as something of a contradiction but in Hudson's case, I submit, it is not. Indeed, one might be forced to confess that for a person of his station he had a not altogether unreasonable hand. The contradiction, if indeed there is one, is substantially explained thus. Hudson's father, named James, was a surveyor who came into Norfolk from Surrey, I believe, with a Board of Ordnance survey party in 1816, or thereabouts, to assist Captain Colby, Colonel Mudge, Lt Charles Bailey and the others in the preparation of a set of one-inch charts commissioned by the Army, which had wisely seen a need for them at the time of the difficulty with France. It was not an easy commission, and there were evidently numerous problems of triangulation because of a scarcity of high places in Norfolk, but they did eventually turn out some tolerable drawings which were not, however, ready for printing until about 1838.

Thomas, having been born in 1782, was already married at this time, and when his father was taken ill and duly expired, he and his wife moved from Surrey, where Thomas had been in the cattle trade, and came to Norfolk to live with his mother, who was also somewhat frail, she herself having been smitten in her youth by the smallpox but having somewhat marvellously recovered, for she had once been ill with cowpox, and this, so it was said, is what saved her. She was a dairymaid in her younger days - in this matter I yet again rely on the evidence of others - and a woman of considerable intellectual achievement. Thus both parents set out to instruct their two sons (Thomas's brother died before either had reached their tenth birthday) not only in the ways of the world but also in reading, writing and numbers, subjects and skills which became particularly important to him later in life.

Following the subsequent death of his mother, Hudson and his wife duly settled at Hempstead, taking on a cottage and a few acres which for most of the year the two of them worked. In about 1819 Thomas, perhaps because of his family's unsettled background in the military, decided that a stationary life was not for him, and he went back to his old profession, that of drover. He was ideally suited to it, and rapidly fashioned a reputation for being one of the most reliable and trustworthy in Norfolk. The town of Holt had long been a stance, or resting place, on the way to St Faith's and was well used to the ways of drovers and their herds, and Hudson was ideally placed at Hempstead to obtain business, leaving home each June or July to head north while his wife brought in their modest harvest, with others, as best she could. Hudson specialised in bringing the black Scottish runts from Dumfries to Fay's Fair, which he did every year for many years, and it was upon this specialisation that he built his knowledge and reputation, for he was known and respected by all the other drovers, by bankers who gave him considerable financial credit, and by the landowners who entrusted him with their herds.

What particularly intrigues me is the manner of his demise, his fall from grace, and the circumstances surrounding it, for I confess I acquired the journal of his final 1829 drove many years ago when his meagre possessions were sold. At about the same time, and for no particular reason other than curiosity and a desire to embrace and record all matters of local historical and antiquarian interest, I also copied the 1833 adjudication findings from the official records. Inevitably, I eventually forgot all about both of them as the years passed and as more pressing matters caught my attention.

April the 5th
Today, being a tolerable sort of day with pale sunshine and a pallid warmth in the air, resolved to walk to the Post Office in High Street to fetch my mail, but on Fish Hill was greatly delayed and mildly agitated by the presence of one Fiddy, an invariably annoying acquaintance who, knowing my reputation in matters archaeological and historical, resolved to puncture it by insisting on raising, yet again, the matter of the irregular shape and construction of the little plain outside my house. Was it not, he insisted, the result of dispute and confrontation, of neighbourhood boundary disagreements and attempted compromise? Yet again I carefully explained to him its original use as a market, and the former stalls positioned thereupon, and that following the conflagration of 1708 the area was reconstructed with buildings replacing the stalls in precisely the same positions.

Yes, yes, yes, he exclaimed, clearly unconvinced; but if that was the case why did the builders build so messily, and why did they not tidy the boundaries to create an area of greater visual pleasure and convenience?

I retorted that perhaps the stallholders had to build on the very places for which they held a stall licence, or for which they had paid their market toll, and that visual pleasure was merely in the eye of the individual. Furthermore, I was quite content, thank-you, with my immediate surroundings, and I also had a pressing engagement.

Fiddy said good-day, somewhat short in temper, and huffed away. Wretched man. To compound my displeasure and ill mood there was not a single letter of any consequence awaiting me at the Post Office, but at least during the walk back I did recall I had done nothing with Harcourt's pieces, and indeed, had irritatedly swept them off my desk some days ago and deposited them on a side table, whereupon they had been completely forgotten.

Later

Retrieved Harcourt's pieces and examined them. Emily had washed and dried them very carefully so that they were clean and wholesome to the touch, and I spread them over my desk and sorted them into separate piles. Thus I was to discover there were three fragments of oyster shell, which are retrieved regularly in these localities and emphasise, I think, a Roman partiality for this sort of sea food; two rather fine examples of roof tile, with traces of some sort of binding material on the corner of one of them; four fragments of the usual coarse grey Roman kitchen ware pottery; two somewhat eroded coins, possibly from the Severus period (though I must consult the appropriate authority for confirmation), which is relatively late; and two pieces of pottery possibly from a box shaped drainage pipe which had been decorated on one side by a workman using a blunt instrument, or even a stick.

He had drawn the tool across the wet clay to create a series of roughly parallel horizontal lines, and then repeated the pattern with vertical strokes, and I could still see where the clay, while wet, had oozed slightly amid the runnels while some had clung to the tool and redeposited itself elsewhere to create a sharp, slightly raised pattern.

However, by far the most interesting of the pieces was a small cube of chalky substance, smoothly worked and clearly cut to shape, which put me in mind immediately of tessera. Once again it reinforced a feeling that somewhere in the area scoured by Harcourt is a substantial building, or buildings. I resolved to write to him, to communicate my views, but for a long time was distracted by the question of how the Romans managed to transport live oysters over long distances and distribute them in such numbers.

It is a subject requiring much thought, and is surely worthy of an essay. In the meantime, I am also determined to give thought to the question of whether the Roman, for defence, or perhaps for better farming practice, preferred the higher ground to the wet valley bottoms, and whether he was naturally drawn to our lofty location, much of which is chalk covered by gravel. There is much to deliberate. Will communicate with Harcourt by letter in the morning.

Afternoon

News of another defeat in the War, God forbid. We lost 30 officers, 500 men, over 100 waggons and 1000 rifles. When is it all to end?

Wednesday, April 21

After breakfast, and in good spirits, strolled churchwards between the trees and spent some time admiring the daffodils that carpet the graveyard to such wonderful effect this year. The interior of the church seemed gloomy in comparison, thanks to the recent restoration, but the rector told me that on days such as these he invariably drew spiritual succour from the light through the stained glass windows and the glowing colours which seem to change hour by hour.

We discussed the election, which has left the Liberals with a majority over the Conservatives of 137 seats, and the Irish Nationalists in possession of no fewer than 65 seats. Gladstone will no doubt form a Liberal ministry with himself as Chancellor of the Exchequer, but we disagreed as to possible choice of Foreign Secretary, a most important role at such an unsettled and critical time. I felt Granville should be given the job, but Brumell thought Chamberlain the better man. As for Bradlaugh, the new Member for Northampton, who has announced he will decline to take the oath, we both agreed the man should be denied entry to the Commons and a new ballot held to decide the seat. It does seem to me some people deliberately cause the most extraordinary dislocation just at a time when our brave soldiers need to know the country is wholly behind them.

Lent Brumell my copy of a small pamphlet recently published on Samuel Rowbotham's Flat Earth theory which purports to show the world is a horizontal disk surrounded by ice, for which the rector expressed his thanks as I know certain immature members of the congregation had spoken in favour of the theory, which seems to me silly in the extreme. He said he would read it with considerable interest and that if the matter persisted as a subject of widespread discourse he might decide to sermonise upon it. I told Brumell I thought Rowbotham quite mad, even the extent to which he had experimentalised on the Old Bedford Level by using a telescope held just above the water. Because he could see barges along the whole six-mile stretch he produced this as proof of his silly theory. Brumell concurred and said he thought Rowbotham, otherwise known as the writer Parallax, might have been better served talking to an American pedestrian named Payson who is walking around England and whom he, Brumell, evidently observed last year in East Dereham. While visiting his friend the local priest, Armstrong by name, Brumell said there was much excitement in the town with crowds awaiting the arrival of this man, Payson, who had walked the 27 miles from King's Lynn. Later, Brumell said, Payson walked on to Lowestoft that same night having visited Norwich and Yarmouth on the way and lectured in both places. The rector joked that as far as he knew Mr Payson was still walking and had still not fallen off the rim of the world.

Rowbotham, Darwin, electricity, Bradlaugh, Cetywayo. God forgive us, we live in changing and disturbing times. Reached home to be informed by Emily that Harcourt had delivered yet another bag of objects.

Sunday

Brumell's sermon today on politics and morality. Rather dry, I thought. My dear wife unable to attend church as she was sorely affected by a bad throat and some sweating. The doctor to visit tomorrow. Emily and cook busily preparing broth, poultices and restoratives.

Monday

My dear wife recovered sufficiently to receive visitors. Promised her we will enjoy an excursion to Cromer as soon as she is well enough and the weather has a touch of warmth. The air might do her good. Sent the ostler's boy to stop the doctor from attending, as we did not require him.

April the 28th

Walked through town to see young Ellis, the bookseller in High Street, to charge him with the task of purchasing two or three titles for me which I have long coveted, including an 1857 Tennyson and Lady Willoughby's Diary of 1844. Also required him to seek out a title by a Yorkshire cleric, Surtees, published at about the same time as the Tennyson, or a little after, which apparently claimed Caesar did not land his troops in Kent, or Richborough, as is popularly and widely held, but on the shores of Norfolk. I look forward to distilling the evidence of Mr Surtees. Ellis, in conversation, praised the prettiness of the Tennyson greatly and recalled the considerable success of Mr Charles Dickens' Pickwick Papers in 1837, published as a part issue, large octavo, paper covered, and distributed to the purchaser rather than the borrower. Serial parts were a publishing fad for upwards of 30 years, I seem to recall, though I had little to do with them. Father always beseeched me to remember that a book was only a book when you could feel its proper weight on your palm and its leather cover on the tips of your fingers.

Sunday

A note from Harcourt yesterday, delivered by some urchin, saying it would not be possible for him to bring me more objects, at least for several months, as the crops are so advanced in their growing that the soil was all but covered. Once the harvest is gathered, he wrote, and the plough teams are on the fields, he will resume his customary interest (though I would describe it as an obsession) in walking the furrows and picking up pieces. The news leaves me strangely unaffected as I am torn between the irritating frequency of the man's calls, the regular appearance of little piles of pottery and whatnots on my desk, and the thought that one day he might find lying on his land something of genuine archaeological value and interest. Decide to return him a note expressing my cautious thanks for his efforts, simply to maintain a communication between us.

This morning, church, but Brumell away and the service taken in his place by some visiting preacher or other.

Afternoon, a visit from Emily, speaking on cook's behalf, to say that work to the window frames in the kitchen and scullery, which we thought of calling workmen to repair last year, had not been done and now the woodwork was sore rotting and letting in the damp. A trifling matter which, as I told Emily in no uncertain terms, my dear wife would deal with as soon as she was harty enough to assume her normal household responsibilities.

Weather unusually bright today, and quite a feeling of spring, which was most pleasing.

Tuesday
Strolling through the market place this morning, and enjoying the pleasant bustle of the place, I was suddenly reminded of Crawley, the land agent involved in the Thomas Hudson affair, and it was only when I returned home, repaired to my study and read all of my notes that I realised I have not hitherto recounted in my commonplace book the incident which brought the entire business to mind in the first place. In a sense, therefore, this is an erratum, or more properly perhaps, an addendum. The fact is that it occurred some time ago in, of all places, Shirehall Plain, where the climax to the Hudson affair also occurred all those years ago, and it was made the more sudden and unexpected because the author of the incident tapped me on the shoulder as I was pausing to admire the water tower.

Having had a tolerable morning with my lawyer discussing business, and my affairs, and feeling particularly sharp in mind and keen in body, quite naturally I turned quickly to confront the perpetrator of this gross impertinence only to find it was the odious Mr Cracknell, manager of our local bank. Cracknell touched his hat and greeted me with a slight bow, but I regarded him somewhat stiffly and made him aware of my displeasure through my demeanour. From that moment the conversation went something like this:

"My dear Mr Hume, what a pleasure. What a particular pleasure."

"Yes?"

"How is Mrs Hume? Well, I trust?"

"Tolerable, thank you."

"You must ensure she keeps herself warm, for the weather remains unusually brisk, do you not think?"

"Yes I do, and it is."

My annoyance at his impertinent approach was still uppermost in my mind. Cracknell, I should explain, was bank under-manager for many years while the honourable Mr Wilby was in charge, and it was Mr Wilby most town gentlemen dealt with. Cracknell was looked upon as almost common, certainly a most unpleasant individual, and there was widespread dismay among the upper circles of Holt society when he was actually appointed manager at the onset of Wilby's ill health and subsequent confinement. No one liked him; nor do they still, even though he has been in the position for several years. Indeed, I happen to know that several important gentlemen have transferred their accounts to Norwich banks simply to be out of the clutches of the man. But that is by the by.

"Do please excuse my unorthodox approach, Mr Hume, but I have been wanting to speak to you for some considerable time, and as you have not been to the bank of late I decided to take advantage of our unsolicited meeting. I have something of interest for you."

"And what would that be?"

I was still extremely affronted by his action, and determined to let him glean the fact.

"A box. Of papers. In fact, several small boxes of papers. They are, as we speak, being gathered together at the bank."

"And of what possible interest are they likely to be to me?"

"You are our most important local historian, are you not? You are interested in local matters and incidents, are you not?"

"Indeed."

"Then I perceive you will be interested in these. They relate to the Crawley affair, and to the drover Thomas Hudson."

"In what way?"

"They are the bank's papers, Mr Hume."

"How could I possibly be allowed to become interested in private papers belonging to the bank, and presumably, at least one of its customers?"

"Mr Hume, the Crawley and Hudson affair was nearly fifty years ago, and none of the participants are alive. Also, none of the papers are in any way relevant to the present smooth running of the bank. On my instructions, the staff have been cleaning out the vault of late and these boxes of papers were examined briefly, deemed to be irrelevant, and were about to be consigned to the flames. Then I recalled your well known fascination with the affair. If you would like to have them, perhaps to research the matter further, then you may do so with the full blessing of the bank, for they represent no more than a hindrance and a clutter to us."

"You have rekindled my interest in the matter."

"Then you would like the papers?"

"Yes. Thank you."

"On the contrary, thank you Mr Hume, for it has relieved us of a disposal problem. I will have them delivered to your home in due course."

And with that the little man bobbed once more, turned, and waddled off. I watched him disappear in the direction of High Street, and then sauntered home wondering if I had done the right thing. All this, of course, was some time ago. Well, early this afternoon Cracknell was as good as his word, for his man arrived at the door with his trap carrying three boxes. The ostler's boy and Emily helped him carry them upstairs and the boxes now sit on the floor in a corner of my study. I cannot think they will reveal much of value and it may be some time before my desk is sufficiently clear to deal with the matter. But I confess I am intrigued.

Monday, May 3
Cook has decided to leave us after two years, complaining she cannot withstand any longer the draught from the window, but we suspect it is for another post - we know not where - presumably because she has been offered more money. My dear wife is distraught at the thought of having to interview and appoint a replacement. But we shall manage. Dear Emily will take care of us, in the meantime, I am sure.

May 17
We are returned from a short holiday much refreshed from the many changes of scenery, fresh air, and the new faces we have seen. Happy to record, it was all a considerable success, and I am content to think that I was the instigator and architect of it. First we visited Norwich, staying at the Maid's Head Hotel, most comfortably, so that we were able to walk to view the livestock market, which was mainly cattle - many of the Devon and Scottish breeds, I noticed - sheep and horses. Very noisy and bustling, and a passing reminder, should one be required, of the sound of bellowing cattle, blowing straw, the hazard of copious amounts of mire (which the old men call tad) about the streets, and the common cheerfulness of raucous humanity, such as we used to experience in Holt up to a few years ago.

We also visited the new Foundry Bridge, built a year or two ago, which my dear wife had not seen before. It is pleasing to think that wools pour into our county from elsewhere by land and sea, and that worsteds from our dear capital city are sent to Russia and Spain, Italy and Turkey, and indeed all over the world. What a nation of traders we are! While my dear wife visited her usual glovers in Golden Ball Street and her milliners in Elm Hill, to arrange delivery, I was able to spend some time looking over the latest book titles in Jarrolds & Sons in London Street, and Matchett &

Stevenson in the Market Place, purchasing one or two of the more sensible and responsible works on display.

Near one entire afternoon was devoted to calling upon an aged aunt of my dear wife who lives in Pottergate, where there is much new building and restoration work going on to the aggravation of pedestrians, and who no more knew us from Adam nor why we were there. The companion told us aunt had good days and bad days, and I can only pray that our arrival happened to coincide with one of her bad days. The visit seemed interminable because Aunt's companion insisted we take tea with them, and so we became involved in a series of conversations about people we knew not and situations which were quite fresh to our ears. Aunt did not even come to the door when we left, but wandered distractedly into the garden saying she had some visitors to see, but her companion, who was at least in possession of most of her faculties, and who did her very best to fulfil the role of hostess, said we were not to worry and that she would care for aunt to the best of her ability. My dear wife, who was filled with compassion, said she was pleased we had visited as aunt, despite her peculiarities, had always had a special place in her heart.

On the third day we travelled by the railway from Norwich to Cromer, which was a particular pleasure, though my dear wife was somewhat apprehensive beforehand as she has never claimed a liking for such a means of travel. Nevertheless, I confess I found the entire experience exhilarating, thoroughly enjoying our splendid procession through Thorpe, Wroxham and North Walsham before arriving at the new Cromer High Station, which turned out to be quite as good as its word, for it afforded a handsome panorama of the village and its neighbourhood, and the sea. We stayed at Lower Tucker's Hotel, preferring it to the Belle Vue, and found it far from crowded and the restaurant tolerably good.

For three days, the weather remaining fair and for the most part sunny, we strolled the cliff path, savoured the air, visited the church which has an exceptionally fine, high tower, observed the coal vessel Wensleydale, and others, bringing trade from Newcastle and the Baltic, and though we did not partake in bathing ourselves, watched some of the more hardy young folk who were moved to take advantage of the brine and the bracing breeze. It was altogether quite pleasant, and indeed, the entire holiday would have been recalled as a complete success had it not been for an annoying altercation with a driver over a hired trap which conveyed us some distance from our hotel to the Lion's Mouth, a most splendid and picturesque tree-lined lane leading to nearby parkland. The man was intolerably rude and I decided there was no alternative but to dismiss him, which I did, but we then had difficulty in engaging an alternative means of transport back to Cromer.

My dear wife was quite exhausted with the anxiety of it all, and the walking, and after returning to Lower Tucker's she took to her room and did not appear for dinner, saying she preferred to rest and read. So I dined alone. In the morning, though, she seemed moderately well and quite cheerful. The following day, being Friday, and quite determined not to allow the incident to spoil our holiday, we spent a long time on the beach watching the sea and engaging the crab fishermen in conversation, and the following day returned home early so we would both be well rested for church on Sunday.

Several years have passed since I was last in Cromer, and I was much taken with the way it had changed since the recent arrival of the steam railway and the railway station. Cromer, during my lifetime, has always been a fishing village and a place where fashionable people could find fresh air, peace and repose, and a place for bathing, and enjoy such dignified rural pleasures as were available. I am reminded, too, that not everyone thought the arrival of the railway was an event to be celebrated on the grounds that the arrival of more and more people, particularly from Norwich, might so alter the quality of an essentially genteel place that it could be spoiled for ever. However, I perceived that Cromer had already changed. For example, the hotel in which we stayed, which was acceptable enough, would not have been built without the imminent arrival of the railway, so it does seem one has to understand that one thing does lead to another and that change, however distressing and painful to some, is a factor of life which cannot be denied. We have to learn to adjust to it, I suppose. I do not know what is the present population of Cromer, but it is quite small, though they do say it will certainly grow in future. In consequence, I am mindful that Holt, situated in our own dear "garden of Norfolk," presently has a population of around 3000 and the prospect of its own railway station in a few years' time. I conclude that change is not only inevitable, it is pressing close all around us.

Later

The new cook has begun work, and although I have not yet been to the kitchen to meet her she is apparently most convivial with Emily, which is a considerable relief. My dear wife seems greatly refreshed in spirit now the whole affair over. Last night at dinner I thought the sirloin somewhat undercooked but decided, in view of my wife's obvious content, not to comment upon the matter.

Saturday, May 22, 1880

Today we had Florence and her husband Hector visit us, but I excused myself early from the sitting-room gossip, not being particularly fond of these friends of my dear wife, saying I had important errands, and thus slipped out of the back door into the town. Emily saw me as I was about to depart, but I raised a finger to my lips to signify that silence would be appreciated, and she simply smiled and went about her business.

This business of change has been troubling me since our return from Cromer, but I suppose it is something to do with a realisation that old age is now upon me, and that I crave the comfort of reassurance. Sat in the church for a time, in my usual pew just beside the font, enjoying the silence, and then decided to stroll home, only to meet the rector coming towards the church, so we sat together on a seat in the churchyard.

I asked him about change, and if everything changed.

"The world changes, time changes, and people change. But God's love does not change," he said.

If the world is changing, why does God's love not have to change, too?

"God's love is the rock," he replied. "It is the one unchanging thing in this world. That is why it is known as the rock."

I suggested that perhaps change was some sort of test set before us by God to see if we could understand it, be at peace with it, and so that we might see more clearly and easily that His love was the only unchanging matter. Brumell was kind enough to concur. But almost immediately, and as though to prove there are other things which do not change, either, he was hailed from the other side of the church yard by another parishioner who clearly sought conversation with him, and he rose to go.

By the way, he said in passing, Mr Fiddy had been to see him about the carstone question again, and he, meaning Fiddy of course, was contemplating a correspondence with the Editor of the Eastern Daily Press on the matter. Did I have any further thoughts on the subject? He would welcome inspiration on the subject before he spoke to Mr Fiddy again. I promised to think about it and communicate my thoughts, but a feeling of deep melancholy continued to weigh on my shoulders all the way home, though passing Ellis's bookshop, which was closed, the mood was lightened somewhat by the sudden thought that perhaps I should contemplate a short vignette on the subject of Hudson and Crawley, and the drove of 1829, so that the matter might not be forgotten entirely.

Evening

In the matter of the church building and the carstone fragments, which are clearly visible in the west facing of the tower, and around which Fiddy has fashioned yet another verbal weapon with which to berate me, the relevant facts, from my knowledge, would appear to be these. In about 1306 the Lady Petronilla, daughter of Sir John de Vaux and wife of Sir William de Nerford, became patron of St Andrew's, and she installed Thomas of

Shotesham as priest. Shortly afterwards, or perhaps even the same year, she ordered the construction of the west tower, and other improvements, including the provision of a new window with stone tracery and the lifting of the nave roof towards the height and proportions we see today, though it must also be remembered that Butterfield also made many further improvements in 1863 following repairs after the alarming conflagration of 1708 which produced such heat the church roof was destroyed, the lead quite melted, and some stone floors cracked. As for the pieces of carstone, Fiddy maintains they represent re-used fragments culled from an old Saxon church, but I have never totally shared his enthusiasm for such a romantic notion.

Following my conversation with Brumell I duly listed some of my objections to Fiddy's unproven notion, among them the realistic thought that the very first church may well have been constructed of timber; that there is no evidence the later church was built, even partly, of carstone; and thus no evidence the fragments in the west tower were re-used pieces acquired during Petronilla's day.

It is worth mentioning there is no stone extant in Holt and therefore stone had to be brought in not only by Petronilla in the 14th century but also following the 18th century repair work following the town fire, and again during Butterfield's improvement of 17 years ago. The truth of the matter is that Holt lies on a ridge of higher ground which extends inland from Cromer and which seems to comprise mainly chalk, sand and gravel. As I have surmised, there is little substantial building material to be obtained here. Carstone, on the other hand, is restricted to a belt which runs south from Hunstanton and through King's Lynn. Why would they bring in carstone, which is known as a weathering stone and not entirely suitable for the building of churches? It is much more likely the builders purchased supplies of proper stone from elsewhere, and further afield, brought the loads in by water as close to Holt as they could, and then overland. If Petronilla's builders did make use of carstone fragments then perhaps the pieces were simply laying around, the residue of some other, smaller enterprise. I shall mull the matter over further and let Brumell know the result of my deliberations.

Wednesday
Yesterday there was a most uplifting occasion of which we were honoured to be a part, and yet, sad to relate, the evening ended in domestic discord with myself very much ill at ease with my dear wife who was, and indeed still is, greatly displeased with me. It was a most unfortunate business. My dear wife and I had graciously accepted an invitation to attend a soiree at the Shire Hall, a prestigious affair to be attended by all the impor-

tant people of the town, and indeed the neighbourhood, and we had spent much of the day preparing for the occasion. Emily had pressed and laid out my dear wife's most fashionable gown, which she had obtained in Norwich on some earlier visit and in which, I thought, she looked particularly handsome, while I had laid out my best evening wear attire, scarf, gloves and top hat. During the afternoon my dear wife asked in passing if we were to be conveyed to the soiree, but I replied quite reasonably that as the weather was fine and the distance between Fish Hill and Shire Hall Plain so short we might stroll and take in the air and thus enjoy the occasion more fully. My suggestion was not entirely welcomed as I now believe she had set her heart on being driven there, but nothing more was said of the matter until shortly before we were due to leave by which time, of course, it was not possible to order even a chaise. Then Emily announced that in the course of her duties she had been into the garden and noticed the weather had changed and it was now drizzling with rain. This was most unfortunate, for even with the assistance of cloaks and umbrellas it still meant we would have to walk through wet streets and arrive somewhat damp. And this is precisely what occurred. What contrived to make the situation worse was the fact that the pavements had indeed become wet and this, together with so many horses and carriages arriving in the Plain, disgorging their passengers and then departing, also meant the roadways were so mired that the hems of my dear wife's skirts became, to her increasing distress, considerably soiled.

At one stage she announced she could certainly not appear at an important public function in such a state, or even proceed further, and that she would prefer to return home, but, eager to attend myself, I talked her into believing no one would notice the state of her hems and that, in any event, the soil would dry in the warmth. Finally she did agree to continue, but her mood and demeanour were fixed for the entire evening, and it was plain she did not enjoy herself, finding relaxation completely beyond her to the extent that she was most strained with me on our eventual return home and, alas, did not speak to me at all this morning.

That business apart, I have to record it was a most glittering occasion, replete with musical entertainment, which was very pleasing. Two of our Justices were in attendance, along with Pemberton, Gurney, two of the Boyds, and the Suffields, of course, all in their finest regalia, all at their most convivial, and a number of most pleasing compliments were paid to me. Late in the evening I spoke to Ballachey, who was conversing somewhat engagingly of concerts he had attended in London over the last year or two. Being interested in the subject I asked if there was a new Beethoven on the horizon, and he assured me there was, for only last year he had attended a Saturday Concert at Crystal Palace at which the main item was a new symphony by Villiers Stanford, which had attracted his attention. He might be the new English Beethoven but for one small matter. "Stanford was born in Dublin," he said, an aside which amused everyone greatly. But were there no others, I asked despairingly? And he went on to mention Sullivan, Sterndale Bennett, Cowen, Benedict and Davenport, which suggested our music was invigoratingly alive, though Stanford, in his opinion, was the more interesting.

Later, as we walked home, I relayed this conversation to my dear wife, knowing her interest in matters musical, but she said nothing and maintained her silence until our return home, whereupon she shouted at Emily that her health had been compromised and that she required a hot balsam brought to her in bed.

Next evening
Our relations being improved not one little jot, my dear wife and I sat in distressing silence throughout what I considered a most tedious and miserable dinner both in atmosphere and sociability, of which there was precious little, and in the manner of the dishes, for which I cared little. What tiny appetite I had beforehand had quite vanished before the end of the soup course. Then my dear wife retired earlier than usual, leaving me to peruse the newspaper and stroll briefly in the garden. Passing the dining-room on the way to my study, and seeing Emily clearing away the dishes, I thought I saw her cast me a not entirely unsympathetic smile; but it was probably nothing.

May 28, being Friday
Spent most of the morning working at correspondence in front of my open study window, which was pleasant, the weather having become most clement again. Occasionally I paused in my task to listen to the outside sounds penetrating my sanctum - fragments of largely meaningless conversations, children's laughter, horses' shod feet scraping the coggles, and the rattle of wheels as a dray or waggon crossed Fish Hill or entered Bull Street. Friendly, comforting sounds. Once an errand boy strolled by whistling Abide With Me, which gave unexpectedly intense pleasure. That so simple and endearing a melody could influence such an innocent mind nurtured much contemplation, and I considered mentioning the matter to Brumell, who might have seen merit in it for the purposes of the pulpit, but when the boy returned later he was whistling another tune which I believe is called I'll Take You Home Again, Kathleen, I having heard it around the piano, though goodness knows where he might have learned it.

Relations with my dear wife marginally improved. At least, we breakfasted together amicably. During the course of some quite aimiable conversations I tactfully pointed out I had not been personally responsible for the rain on the evening of the Shire Hall soiree, which was the contentious matter between us, and she, I believe, accepted my point of view.

Complained to Emily the kidneys somewhat underdone and she said she would mention it to cook. My dear wife appeared not to hear my plaint, or at least, declined to say anything.

Evening
Regarding Harcourt's latest artefacts and my suspicion there may once have existed a Roman villa in the vicinity of his farm, my mind is beginning to allow the possibility of some link between this and the earthworks of the Danish Camp at Warham St Mary. Note: can dating problem be resolved?

Saturday
Secker, my gardener, here this morning, the weather remaining handsome, and so walked with him around the beds and paths and assisted in several small ways, offering advice where I felt it was necessary. He removed suckers from the roses, a task I scarcely ever draw pleasure from, lifted and divided the primroses and polyanthus, planted out the pelargoniums and picked sweet peas for the house. He seemed quite content when I paid him and doffed his cap most courteously. Then he said, most solitiously and politely, he had been puzzling over my initials, TWH, which he had evidently seen somewhere, and so explained I was christened Thomas Westcott Hume, Thomas being a traditional Hume family name, Westcott being my mother's maiden name, she having been of a good family which hailed from Huntingdon. Secker seemed most interested, and thanked me lavishly.

Later, it being so pleasant, my dear wife and I sat for some considerable time in a bosky portion of the garden near the buddleia, and watched the butterflies, and rejoiced in the beauty and variety of God's handiwork.

A most interesting conversation at dinner. My dear wife recorded she had been given the details of a female - should the person concerned actually warrant the name - who had been seen using tobacco quite wantonly and openly in the street, a scandalous occurrence the like of which I hope I shall never witness. This was in Hempstead road. The news has evidently quite distressed members of my dear wife's circle of lady acquaintances. I replied that as reprehensible as it might have seemed it was as nothing set against the silliness of the new fad for bicycling. Several of these contraptions with wooden wheels, iron tyres, and seats so high one fears for the safety of the rider, have been seen in the town, and I myself saw one only two days' previously along the Cromer road. That dreadful nuisance Fiddy told me some time ago he had seen a participant fall from one of these contraptions, owing to the poor state of the roads hereabouts. For myself, I cannot see the advantage of them, for if exercise and fresh air is the aim then it seems to me a daily perambulation around the town is all that is needed, and the best possible exercise.

Beef course the most ill cooked I have ever come across. Decided to say nothing on account of my dear wife's delicate demeanour, but left most of it on my plate so that my displeasure should be registered.

Sunday
At church, Brumell preached on the usefulness of persistence and tenacity, citing the example of Webb swimming the English Channel. A colourless sermon, I thought. Saw Fiddy among the congregation, and we nodded to each other.

Afternoon
Had previously accepted an invitation to visit the family of X, the wife being a distant relation of Viscount Canterbury, president of the Norfolk Club, so we were driven to Hindolveston by the ostler's boy in a hired chaise from The Angel, to X's passably fine house not far from the beck. A most pleasant interlude, and my dear wife in excellent humour throughout. Main purpose of the visit was a special view of their recently acquired painting by John Berney Ladbrooke, titled Water Lane, Autumn, actually painted, so I believe, some 20 years ago. They had it hanging in the drawing-room, and very handsome it was, too. I particularly liked the fine detail of the foliage. Ladbrooke, poor fellow, died last year. Knew him slightly when he resided in Thorpe Hamlet, at a house on the heights, and when he earned remuneration by giving drawing lessons. Returned home considerably refreshed in mind and body, having been entertained most civilly.

Monday
Today spent several hours reading, though completely without pleasure or concentration as my mind greatly troubled by an incident during breakfast of which, I am sure, I was the innocent and inadvertent instigator. I had been contemplating with considerable pleasure the prospect of haddock, as is my wont on Monday mornings, and on finding none on the table expressed my disappointment and quite naturally required of Emily an explanation. She replied that cook had provided none, so I prevailed upon Emily to visit the kitchen for an explanation and she, brave girl,

immediately returned with cook's somewhat impertinent comment that if haddock was not available then none would be supplied. This seemed to me to be a direct criticism of the way my dear wife - who leads a distressingly busy life quite burdened with household and social responsibilities - oversaw the ordering of provisions, which was something I could not accept.

Considerably angered, I dispatched Emily once again to the staff quarters with the message that I always partook of haddock on a Monday and would continue to do so every Monday in the foreseeable future, and that it was cook's responsibility to ensure it was obtained and prepared for the table. Wretched woman; and a most unseemly business. In the meantime my dear wife, who of course abhors distractions and altercations, maintained a dignified silence throughout the episode, for which I was most grateful. But we left table in ill humour.

Later
Brumell is right, after all. Tenacity can oft-times overcome adversity. Unable to concentrate on my book I determined instead to occupy my time with useful labour and to undertake a search for the sheets on which, some years before, I had copied Hudson's 1833 Shire Hall adjudication. It took a considerable effort and much moving of books, which tired me considerably and which, in the main, I discovered to be covered with a thin coating of dust. Resolved to ask Emily to rectify the matter when next she had time free from her other duties. Nevertheless, the sheets finally came to light in an obscure corner of a manuscript cupboard, and I glanced at them with pleasure and a degree of satisfaction. Now I have Hudson's adjudication and Cracknell's papers from the bank, both to hand beside my desk, and more, a refreshing desire to re-examine the entire business of the 1829 drove all over again to see what new information I can glean. There remains only the recovery of Hudson's own journal, which I know to be somewhere in the roof space; and thus I am resolved to retrieve it.

Evening
After dinner, my dear wife having retired early and Emily having cleared away the remnants of the meal, I called her to the landing of the upper floor, first telling her to bring a lantern while I procured the services of a step ladder. Upon her arrival, and while Emily lit the lantern, I placed the ladder against the wall beneath the roof entrance and climbed up and, after some initial difficulty, removed the ceiling door. An unmistakeable smell of warm air and dust assailed my nostrils. Returning to floor level again in order to place the door in a suitably safe position, the brave Emily, holding the lantern, immediately began to ascend the ladder ahead of me,

saying she would light the way. I determined the most useful service I could perform was to stand on the bottom rung of the ladder to prevent it moving suddenly and alarming Emily, and thus it was that I looked up to see what progress she had made, and saw the movement of her gown as she climbed and her remarkably trim feet and slim ankles, and was at once shocked by thoughts of a quite distressing nature which inadvertently entered my mind, and which, of course, I endeavoured to banish immediately.

Once she had achieved the climb and entered the roof space, and the lantern lit the interior so that I could see the timbers of the underside quite plainly, she called to me that the search could now begin, so I climbed - with some trepidation, I might say - into that place of concealment, confinement, warmth, light, and quite innocent intimacy. Emily, being appraised of what it was I sought, searched one end of the roof space and I the other, with the lantern between us, so that as we searched among the chests, boxes, and discarded items of furniture, we moved closer and closer together, until finally, and with a little exclamation of glee, she found the chest I had earlier described to her, and opened it and reached in. Then she lifted up the volume into the light, and I knew immediately it was Hudson's. I thanked her profusely, and together we returned down the ladder and replaced the ceiling door, and it was then I realised I was perspiring mightily, from the heat in the roof space no doubt, while Emily was quite charmingly flushed about the cheeks.

Wednesday, June 2
Hudson's little journal sits on my desk, begging to be read, but I am not yet quite ready. It is a cheap volume with chafed covers and poor quality, unlined paper. His handwriting is varied, some reasonable, some more difficult to read, as it was clearly scribed at speed or in places or conditions of awkwardness.

Thursday, June 3
The morning being very overcast and yet quite dry under foot, took my perambulation across to the church with the intention of finding Hudson's grave. The approach to the church beneath the trees was pleasing, and there were flowers between many of the memorial stones, but all my efforts to find Hudson's last resting place in the area near to the wall to the right of the main door were quite without success, despite an appreciation of the presence of several unmarked graves. Brumell, when I saw him in the church, also quite without information. It was as though Hudson had quite simply vanished from this world without leaving any physical trace.

Told Brumell I had seen Fiddy again, but had no opportunity for conversation.

"Fiddy is a persistent nuisance," he said, with uncharacteristic candour.

My conviction, I told him, was that there was absolutely no evidence of any earlier building constructed from carstone - which must have been brought in by water or by waggon - but that the church builders, or subsequent repairers, might have incorporated in the present church a few remnants they had found laying around, which could have been acquired for some adornment or other, or even as ballast.

"It will not satisfy Fiddy," Brumell retorted, so I promised I would think further around the matter.

I also mentioned the matter and manner of Hudson's journal having come to light again, and Brumell wondered if his vestry documents might provide any further detail on the affair, but thought it unlikely, and then raised the point that whereas the name Holt, or holt, was perceived as meaning a wooded place, or a small plantation, halt was most often seen as also meaning a resting place for cattle. He further proffered the thought that perhaps our little town had long been a magnet for cattle and for the men who looked after them.

Complimented him on the previous Sunday's sermon, and my own subsequent appreciation of the value of perseverence, and suggested that one Sabbath he might consider the question of light as the basis of a sermon, based on the premise that although some people fear the dark, the drovers of old in fact welcomed dark nights, the reason being that in bright moonlight their charges tended to stray. Thus, in moonlight, the drovers were kept constantly occupied in keeping the herd together. He said he would consider the matter and thanked me profusely for such a charming little allegory.

Friday
My mind much preoccupied by the thought that Hudson evidently left no mark, and spent a considerable time wondering if it mattered if we are completely forgotten after we depart to that other sweet shore. Also exercised by the thought that I am in my 67th year, with a dear wife but no family, and thus with no one to leave my life's residue to. The sum total of my earthly riches is modestly considerable, for my father (despite his dissolute youth) and grandfather were most prudent in their dealings and innovative in their decisions, mainly in the paper and printing industry and largely in the production of fine quality writing paper, envelopes, In Memorial cards, greetings cards and other such fancies. I rejoice in the solidity of their business, for they were successful to the extent that I, for

example, have never once had to soil my hands with common or regular toil or labour, save those of an intellectual bent. It has been a great comfort, for I can recall my father once telling me, "A good school is of greater importance than a monied parent." I have had the benefit of both to the extent that my dear wife and I, and our little household, are quite comfortably off. But that does not answer the questions which have consistently populated my mind of late. To whom do I leave my possessions, assuming I outlive my dear wife? Will anyone remember me after I have gone? And if not, does it matter? I must talk to Brumell again.

The same day, late afternoon
A most distressing business. Accosted cook in the kitchen to inform her of my continued displeasure, whereupon the wretch assailed me with quite venomous language. Left with absolutely no alternative I dismissed her immediately and instructed her to leave the house forthwith. Which she did. Upon hearing the noise and raised voices my dear wife arrived on the scene to see the cause of it and just in time to witness cook hurrying out of the tradesmen's door, shaking her fists and bringing forth the most indecent of expressions. Upon appraising my dear wife of the situation, and recounting in detail the fact that I had dismissed cook, and the reasons for my action, my dear wife was stricken by a most theatrical fainting episode after which, on partial recovery, she expressed her great displeasure with me and entreated me to explain where she might obtain a new cook at such short notice. I replied firmly that such matters were outside my area of jurisdiction, and that the matter was up to her. Thus I repaired to my room and closed the door, ordering Emily to bring me my meals here.

Later still
Continue to be disturbed by the distant sound of my dear wife sobbing in her room, but I am quite resolved, and utterly resolute upon my position. To pass the time have begun to re-read and copy Hudson's journal.

Thomas Hudson's Drove

Galloway, Scotland
August, 1829

AT THE place called Rigg where the muddy roads to Gretna and Moorend stretch into the misty and barely visible distance, and a few yards from where a tumble of stones on the stream bank mark the place of the ford which was ancient even before present memory, Thomas Hudson turned his cob into the lee of a tangle of overhanging trees and branches to try to gain some sort of respite from the rain. He slid from the animal's back, gathered the reins, and distractedly tied them to a sprit. Animal and the man both seemed quiet enough, but it was noticeable the two kept eyeing each other, not knowing what to think, as though anticipating some sudden, unexpected movement. Even after a day they were still undecided about the other's intentions. The uncertainty was particularly noticeable at the Annan stream when the animal saw the grey, swollen, white-crested water, and hesitated, pawing at the stones on the sodden ground, and when the rider jabbed his heels into its flanks and urged it forward. The animal was unsure, the rider adamant, and it took more jabs, tugs and urgings before the cob did finally move forward, feeling the freezing water lashing at its shins, splashing its barrel, fretting as its hooves slipped and clattered on the jumbled, uneven carpet of stones somewhere out of sight below the foaming surface. Eventually they did reach the far side, with honours even; yet the uncertainty still remained.

Now as the animal shook itself, sending an arc of freezing droplets spraying into the grey air, and as Hudson looked about him, he became aware of other figures also sheltering from the downpour, pressing themselves back into the foliage a short distance away. An old couple, clutching covered baskets and swaddled in coarse brown blanket-like plaits, with water streaming down their faces. Then he looked at the rain again, which had come on suddenly as he had been riding from Gretna on the road to Dumfries. Banks of grey cloud which had been building all day over the Solway Firth had finally moved inland and shed their load. And it had been incessant for the last two miles, falling with a ferocity that stung the skin, dancing and bouncing on the stones, turning the road into a morass of streaming water.

He knew something unusual had happened. Was happening. Everyone said so. Riding north from Norfolk the weather had become increasingly unsettled, there were strange lights in the sky he had not seen before, and a great deal of rain. And the closer he got to Scotland the worse it seemed to be. A drover in Bowes, heading south with a small herd of listless, tired looking runts, their coats shining with rain and sweaty lather, told him there were huge floods in the valleys and that many bridges had been swept away. Then at Brough, as he ate at the Golden Fleece, there were tales among the damp, leathery, unshaven men of crops and property, stock and trees, all destroyed, and dikes and rivers unable to cope with the torrents. And in Gretna he met a drunken English jagger with a stranded pack train, waiting for fresh animals, who told him it all happened on the night of August 2.

"They say it rained as much in one night as the length of my forearm," he said. "And the wind . . .   That were something terrible. I saw what it did. Shocks flat in the harvest fields, trees down, cottar roofs blowed away."

The man shook his head in bewilderment and then consoled himself by saying he had another two days to wait before his replacement ponies arrived.

Hudson was dressed in his usual slashed waistcoat and hosen breeches with a long, thick frock coat, leather boots and a squashed flat hat, currently greatly favoured by the southern drovers, and one of the trademarks of his profession, and the rain worried him not one jot, for he could always dry off once it had stopped, and then start riding again or doze beside some hostelry fireplace, his clothes steaming in the heat. What concerned him more was the state of the roads, which away from the turnpikes was generally poor, and now flooded more often than not; what he might find in Dumfries; and the condition of the satchel he carried at his waist. It contained his snuff, in a horn box, and his pipe and tobacco, but more importantly his licence, his letters of credit and promissory notes from the bank, for Mr Crawley, and letters of introduction from Mr Porter - by and large the documentation of his trade - and the little book with the blank white pages given to him by his wife for writing in. He ran his fingers down the side of the satchel, feeling the damp leather, and then undid the buckle, lifted the flap and peered inside. A reassuring smell of tobacco wafted upwards, and seeing that the objects and papers were still tightly wrapped, and feeling no dampness anywhere, he re-buckled the flap with a sense of relief.

As soon as the rain began to fall with a little less vehemence the old couple stirred, collected their belongings, the bits and pieces of their life, and, hanging on to each other's arm, finally left the shelter of the trees to continue their slow journey towards Gretna and some unknown, unforeseeable fate. He called out to them to ask of the way ahead, and they said there was much flooding, even in Dumfries. But their voices were thin, alarmed and uncertain. Then they turned away, absorbed in each other, and he watched them for some time until they slowly disappeared in the gloom and round a corner of the road. In truth, he himself was reluctant to begin the journey again, and when he looked at the cob waiting patiently beside him he understood why.

Even this early in the endeavour he sensed the drove had not begun well. There had been an unexpected delay over certain papers at the bank, which had seemed unaccountably fastidious in dealing with the entire transaction, and Mr Porter's inexplicable long prevarication, so that he, Hudson, had been unable to secure his usual men for the enterprise and was having to do with a make-shift team. Then, heading north from Norfolk and a few miles south of Carlisle, his own mare, Jenny, which had been with him to Scotland and back six or seven times and had been his constant and trusted companion on many a drove, began to tell him that all was not well.

There was a lethargy about her he had not seen before, and did not fully understand, and by the time he reached Gretna he suspected it was all up. Jenny was shivering and exhausted, her head low, and not eating. In truth, they could not go on. But because it was Jenny, his friend, he found her a good stable with clean straw and stayed with her, waiting two days. It was to no avail. She was on her feet, but immobile and unhappy and eating little, and in the end he had no option. He found a dealer from Moorend who happened to be in Gretna on business, and he came and looked at Jenny and said he would take her, and offered to let Hudson purchase one of his own choosing from a string he happened to have with him at an inn yard. Hudson collected Jenny and walked with her and the dealer to the yard where he looked for a long time at the mounts available, and finally, and because he could see no other which was better, they did the deal.

The dealer tied Jenny to the rest of the string and Hudson paid for the new animal - a sturdy cob with a docked tail - and rode away without looking back, as though he could no longer look his old friend in the eye. He knew the knacker's yard awaited her, and it was as though he wanted to put the location far behind him, for he left Gretna hurridly in blowing, threatening weather knowing it would rain within the hour. But it was not the thought of rain that bothered him, and urged him on. It was the vision of Jenny facing a bloody, butchered end.

In the end the deluge did begin to die away, and he finally untied the cob and led it back on to the road to the sound, coming from all directions, of running water and the blowing wind. He was no longer cold or numb, but was beginning to fill his mind with the copious details of the forthcoming journey. He had to leave Jenny behind him, just as he had to leave the girl at Boroughbridge far behind him. The memories of both losses filled him with sadness, and forced him to silence and introspection as he rode on.

Near Cummertrees, with darkness descending and a fierce wind blowing off the Firth, he found a dry, secure place for them both and some patchy, scrubby grass for the cob between a thick hedge and the brick wall of an empty creweyard. He gave the animal some oats, which he took from his pack, and then prepared his own meal of dried meat and bread, and when he was finished fetched his pipe and tobacco and found comfort in the aroma of the smoke. It reminded him that one of the roads hereabouts was known as the Tobacco Road. A hundred years ago an imperious Englishman had visited Dumfries and grandly invested heavily in tobacco, which was an important local sea trade at the time, and had then gone away, never, for some reason, to return. Hudson wondered who he was, and if he had died suddenly. In the event, a long time later, and with the tobacco still lying unclaimed in store, the value of the shipment was finally realised, and with no one able to claim it as their own it was spent, instead, on the road. Hence the Tobacco Road.

The tale amused him, and when his pipe was over he pulled his greatcoat around him and slept on the ground happily and deeply, being aware only of the slight occasional stirrings of the cob and the sound of the wind buffeting and bludgeoning the hedgerow.

Next morning, near midday, when the weather was brighter and the banks of racing clouds were piled high, Hudson rode into Dumfries to find White Sands (the riverside where they usually rested and watered the cattle) a shining expanse of floodwater and the Nith bridge swamped, the river lapping over the steps and washing half way along Friars Vennel. Seagulls swooped and called over the waters, while at the edges debris and filth slopped and stank and coated everything in a stinking, squalid mess. He reined in and looked at the scene, fascinated and yet uncertain where to go or what to do, because the landscape had changed. Groups of people stood idly by at the extremities of the water and gazed with utter futility at the great shining flood which had invaded their town, and here and there, to the amusement of the bystanders, yelping dogs chased rats as the creatures vacated their water-filled hiding places and sought dry ground. Then from out of Bank Street a muffled man in a handsome whiskey emerged and attempted to drive towards the bridge. The wheels of the whiskey slushed and splashed through the tide, leaving in their wake a long column of bubbles and disturbed water. But finally thinking the better of it, and with the pony showing signs of alarm, the driver suddenly turned and disappeared back into Bank Street. A bystander called to him as he negotiated the corner, and he laughed and raised a hand in recognition, the sound of their voices echoing across the great shining pool.

Hudson watched for a while and then rode away, further into town, having determined there was a need to purchase hay. But when he found a smiddy, and dismounted and accosted a hulking Scot in the hot inner recesses of his darkly glowing sanctum, the man said in quite unfriendly tones there was no hay in the town, but he might try Gilchrist at the stables. A short time later, at the stables, he heard a similar story. Gilchrist was not there, but his lad, an animated dwarf of a creature who clucked over his words and clung to Hudson's stirrup as he spoke, as though determined not to let him depart, waved his other deformed and foreshortened arm to indicate the empty hay loft and to explain it was all "swep awa i'th wind." The mission seemed hopeless, and after several further attempts to find enough for his mount's needs, and after running to earth nothing more than the valueless sweepings of a largely empty loft behind a dingy inn, and being offered it at a ridiculous price, Hudson decided to turn his attention instead to a bed for the night and a decent stable.

Even before he reached the Hole In the Wall Inn he knew matters were not as they usually were, for there were a pair of four-wheeled chaises and a tilt waggon parked higgledy-piggledy out front, all of them loaded with household pieces and luggage, and a general clamour and hubbub of raised voices. Hudson pushed through the knot of people, determined to seek out landlord Cairncross, and entered the inn. The parlour was full of travellers and farmers, and in the kitchen there were hams and flitches of bacon suspended from the ceiling, and a well scoured table laden with food. Jacks creaked and turned spits as joints of meat piped and smoked before big fires. Shining pots and pans decorated the walls, clocks ticked, and waiters and housemaids scurried to and fro, dodging back and forth round and behind him, seemingly oblivious of his presence.

"Coming, sir."

"Please step this way, ma'm."

"Be with you in a wee moment, sir."

The passage was partially blocked by piles of luggage stacked against the wall, and Hudson had to turn sideways to squeeze passed. Then he saw Cairncross in animated discussion with a family party, with nowhere to sit, standing disconsolately in the doorway to the parlour. He was throwing his hands in the air and shaking his head, but when he saw Hudson he abruptly broke off the conversation and came across. The pair greeted each other like old friends, and shook hands. Then the landlord broke away, his mind full of the frantic misunderstandings and demands of the moment.

"These people," he said, wringing his hands. "They think I have innumerable rooms and limitless space."

"Who are they?"

"Mainly farmers. All sorts. They flee the lowland valleys because of the flooding, and now they want somewhere to sleep."

"You have no-where?"

"No-where. Not even for you, my friend. Not a bench, a chair, or a portion of floor space. Nothing. Everything is taken. I do not even have a bed for myself tonight."

"The Globe?"

He shook his head.

"The Globe is the same. It has been completely full for two days."

Then he leaned his head forwards, conspiritorially.

"I can give you the address of a widow lady, if you wish, who will give you a roof for the night."

He whispered the name and address, and Hudson nodded his thanks. Then the landlord called one of the housemaids from the kitchen and ordered a chop and hot potato and a jar of ale for his friend, and finally disappeared back into the ill-tempered throng. Hudson was grateful. He had known Cairncross for several years. He had always been a decent landlord, fair and insistent on good value, offering a decent whole bed with clean sheets, and the drover had made the inn a port of call on each of his visits to Dumfries. When the girl came with the food and drink she indicated a cramped corner in the noisy, overcrowded parlour where he could place his plate while he ate his meal, and in the middle of the comings and goings, the shouting and arguing, the bumping and banging, he found himself on his own again. His clothes steamed gently in the heat, and there was a general, pervading smell of damp, agitated humanity, mixed with the whiff of smoke, spittle, food and whisky.

Hudson banged on the door of the widow lady sometime later. It was in the corner of a small, squalid and dirty courtyard off Bank Street. The neighbours leaned from nearby windows or stood in their doorways and watched him. When the door finally opened he saw a neatly dressed, timid lady, who glanced away from him at her still staring neighbours and then ushered him hurriedly inside.

The interior was dark, but once his eyes had adjusted he saw the house was sparsely furnished, though there were a few religious prints on the walls. Plain, but well kept and clean. But yes, she had a room, and she could arrange for a nearby stable to take his mount for the night. She told him the price, and as she clumped up the stairs to show him the room she explained, in answer to his question, that her husband, a leather worker, had died suddenly the previous year and so she was obliged to take an occasional guest to pay her way. She had sworn to be a burden to no-one, she whispered, in the manner of a martyr. He sensed in her a degree of self pride, someone who carried a cross, and guessed her family probably thought she had married beneath her. Perhaps she had married for love.

Afterwards, and in as nice a manner as possible, she asked him his business and where he was from, and he told her, but she seemed only mildly interested, in a preoccupied sort of way. Later that evening, before the sun died, Hudson washed himself and hung up his clothes to air in front of an empty hearth, and then rummaged in his satchel for his notebook and spent some time writing. He was slow and careful with his writing, taking time to form the letters properly, but before it finally got dark he was satisfied he had written all he could. Shortly afterwards he went to bed and, luxuriating in clean sheets and the smell of feathers and crisp linen, soon fell into a languid sleep thinking of his wife and the harvest, and warm Betty at the Boroughbridge inn, and Jenny and the knacker at Moorend. Norfolk seemed a long time and a long way away.

Early next morning the urgent sound of knocking at the bedroom door woke him, and he emerged from his befuddled sleep aware of sunlight flooding in through the unadorned, grimy window. The room seemed even more cheerless than the previous day, and his still damp clothes still hung lifeless and unappealing around the hearth. Then he heard the sound of the widow woman's voice.

"There is an urgent message, sir. Brought by an urchin. Sent on by Mr Caircross at the Hole i'th Wall. Shall I leave it for you on the table downstairs?"

"Yes. Thank you."

"Shall I give the urchin a wee coin?" She sounded concerned.

"Yes, please. I will repay you."

"Very well."

He lay and listened as her footsteps scuttled away down the wooden stairs, and then he heard the faraway sound of her voice as she dealt with the urchin at the door.

Hudson did not hurry with his preparations, for after so long on the road he was still enjoying the longed-for pleasures of a roof over his head, a room of his own, and the all-embracing luxury of crisp, white sheets, pillows, and feathers to sleep on. When he did finally clatter down the bare wooden stairs it was to find the house evidently deserted. The letter was on the table, just as the widow woman had said, and he felt the quality of the paper between his fingers, smelled it, purely for the pleasure, and then read the handwriting scribed by what he perceived as a cultured hand.

"Mr Thomas Hudson of Hempstead, Norfolk," it said, "resident at the Hole In The Wall, Dumfries. May I welcome you to Scotland. May I also ask that as soon as is reasonably possible you ride on to The Lodge at Durisdeer, where I am currently in residence, so that we may finalise the business and arrangements of the drove and attend to the details of the tryst. I will be happy to accommodate you at The Lodge for such time as you need before beginning the drove to Norfolk. You will be aware of the capriciousness of the recent weather, and some of the attendant difficulties, and will no doubt appreciate I am anxious to complete the business in haste. With this in mind I have already set certain matters in motion. Signed, Jonathan Crawley, agent for Mr Porter, gentleman farmer, of Blakeney, Norfolk."

He read it through a second time and then folded it carefully between the covers of the notebook, which he placed back in his satchel. Then he paused and considered matters.

He had met Crawley only the once, and then briefly, when he had been summoned to the farm by Mr Porter to be asked if he would take the drove. Mr Porter, a nervous, evidently sickly man, had impressed upon him the financial importance of the drove and the pressing need for good prices at Fay's Fair; but the terms had been good, better than he was likely to get elsewhere all summer, so he had shaken hands without much thought. Only then, after the deal was done, did Mr Porter introduce him to Crawley, the agent. Crawley, a tall, awkward man with a long, cadaverous face and the speech of one who had been properly schooled, stepped forward to introduce himself, shook hands, and then stepped back into the shadows. Now here he was, in residence in Scotland - though he could not bring himself to think Crawley actually owned The Lodge - evidently making certain arrangements for the drove. It was most unusual.

Hudson's train of thought was interrupted by the return of the widow woman who had been to the stable to see after the well-being of the cob. She said it was rested and had been fed and watered, and he thanked her for her concern.

"Where is Durisdeer?" he asked, as he counted out the coins to pay her.

"Yon 20 miles, I'd say. Follow the Nith upstream to Thornhill and then towards the Lowther Hills. You a-going that way? They say the floods are bad."

"I think I must. Do you know who lives at The Lodge there?"

"Noooo . . . I do not. But someone important, I have n' doubt."

"We shall see."

Then he paid her and gave her a few extra coins for her diligence, and stepped across the dismal courtyard and back into Bank Street. It was to find the weather had improved, being breezy and sunny, and the floods had receded slightly, though White Sands was still a slopping, gleaming expanse of rubbish-strewn water.

For a time he wandered the busy streets, past Midsteeple Tower with its mile marker (Huntingdon, 272 miles), sampling the freedom and enjoying the jostle and chatter of shoppers, strollers and business people, the smell of the coffee house and the stench of the flesh market, and he eventually purchased small stores of oatmeal (to cook bannock), and honey and whisky (for the brose). Then he attended The British Linen Bank where he presented his letters of credit to an officious clerk, discussed rates of interest, confirmed the bank would be at the tryst, and duly signed the notes. The bank seemed confident that cattle prices, and thus interest rates, would hold. Despite the floods, the indications were of another reasonable year. Then when he had finished at the bank, and completed his purchases, he fetched his mount from the stables and saddled it, strapping on the loaded panniers. Man and animal eyed each other afresh, revisiting yesterday's feelings of uncertainty and coming to their own unspoken conclusions.

Some way along High Street, walking the horse beside Midsteeple Tower, he became aware of a commotion at the far end of the street and the sounds of shouting and horses' hooves. He stopped and waited, and after a moment recognised the approaching hubbub as the London mail which finally clattered into view and came to a noisy halt, the coachman, red cheeked and ready for a meal beside a welcoming fire, standing up to haul on the traces. The scarlet, maroon and black coach, pulled by four exhausted matching chestnuts, was caked with mud, as were the outside passengers. Water streamed from the wheels and from the heaving flanks of the horses, and even the scarlet uniformed guard had to shake the water from his hat and try to remove some of the mud by wiping himself down with the flat of his hand before he dismounted.

Hudson gleaned from bystanders the coach was late and that there had been some concern about it, but he knew it would encounter better running and drier roads once it got further south.

There were three passengers on top, muffled against the wet and cold, and it was only as they began to clamber down, after the "quality" seated inside had been greeted by the ostlers and stretched their limbs and dispersed, that Hudson realised one of them looked familiar. Despite the greatcoat, with its high collar pulled up above the ears, and the battered, sodden hat, he could still recognise the friendly bewhiskered features of Isaac Swann, a working companion from many a drove. Hudson hailed him, and Swann came across.

"Thomas," Swann said at once, cheerfully and without irony, "I have come to offer my services."

His beard was covered in droplets, his greatcoat dripping water, and mud glistened across his shoulders and back where it had been flung by the turning of the coach wheels. Hudson greeted him with affection and some puzzlement.

"It was my understanding you were travelling up from Norfolk. I did not expect to see you until the tryst."

Swann explained he had been to Glasgow to complete some business for another client from Norfolk, which he had done, but had then found his mount to be lacking in strength for a long, working ride home, and had sold it, catching the mail coach instead.

"I heard you were working here, and decided to come to find you, to see if I might ride with you and the herd," he explained.

They wandered away from the chattering crowd around the coach and team, and moved a little further along the street where there was more space and less noise.

Hudson was pleased to have him, just as he knew many business people were anxious to engage him, because of Swann's respectable and reliable reputation.

"You may indeed," he said, "and you may also earn yourself some coins by joining the drove. It is still within my domain to choose the team. We leave as soon as possible after the tryst."

"I need a horse, so I will purchase one here and join you as soon as I can."

Hudson nodded and then explained about Porter and Crawley, and the letter, and his imminent departure for Durisdeer.

"Refresh yourself overnight, find a mount, and ride towards Durisdeer when you are ready. You have coins enough?"

Swann nodded. "Enough," he said, "and for oatmeal. I will join you again as soon as I can. And thank you."

Hudson was much cheered by the finding of a familiar face, and this face in particular. He trusted Swann, the younger man, who was born in Holt and who had proved time and again to be a resourceful ally on many a long road home. Then he asked him of the road north of Dumfries.

"It is bad in places, but not impassable, and it will begin to dry if the weather decides to hold fair. The ground is sodden, but the herd will keep moving."

"White Sands is flooded."

"I'm not surprised. I've not seen such rains before as fell earlier in the month. There are so many rivers over their banks. You will have to take the herd through the town."

"When is market day?"

Swann said it was every Wednesday.

"Then we will go through the middle of Dumfries, but not on a Wednesday or on the Sabbath," Hudson replied, nodding sagely.

The pair parted amicably, both of them cheered by the accidental meeting, and Hudson continued to walk his mount along High Street as Swann wandered off in the other direction to find a meal and a bed for the night. In the middle of the crowd milling around Midsteeple Tower, a Boots and two helpers unloaded and sorted the mail coach luggage while two ostlers struggled to change the sweating, impatient team. Then, shortly before noon, Hudson walked with the cob through the ankle-deep water over the Nith bridge and headed north towards the cloud-topped range of the Lowther Hills glowering in the background.

There were few other people on the road despite a distinct feeling, which he could not describe, that the rain might at last have paused in its onslaught. At least there was an element of warmth in the sun. Once, he was passed by a scowling, black-cloaked cleric on an aged cob who nodded and said nothing, and whose face scarce altered a line of its permanently etched frown. And twice he saw defeated looking labourers walking slowly towards Dumfries, heads down and loads dragging, their feet trailing through the mud and puddles. And once, before he reached Thornhill, a lightly-laden and yet still slow moving diligence hauled painfully by a straining team hove into view. There were three men with the vehicle, but they, too, said nothing and communicated nothing beyond a brief nod of recognition, and Hudson surmised the load and wet roads had been too much for the team and they had been forced to leave much of their regular load behind, or store it safe somewhere.

With the practised ease of a man who could read the landscape, and knew its vagaries, he kept to the east side of the Nith river, and well away from it, for he knew it to be badly swollen in places. The landscape rolled gently in front of him and there were rocky outcrops on some of the gentle crests. Later, as the shape of the hills slowly emerged ahead of him out of the mist and cloud, and grew ever larger, he began to ride through hilly valleys and splash over innumerable running streams where he knew there should not be streams at all. In Gatelawbridge, a miserable village on a small plateau surrounded by the hills, there was little activity and few signs of life save for a few cottars standing silently in their doorways, no doubt contemplating the sodden landscape and the consequent lack of work, and it was with some relief that he left it behind. A few miles further on, and having decided he and his mount both needed a rest, he stopped beside the looming walls and iron gate of a Church of Scotland burial chapel. It was a grim place, to his eyes. The chapel was dark, closed and silent, raindrops dripped from the surrounding trees, and what few stones there were in the graveyard glistened with wet and the clinging grasp of moss . While the cob grazed nearby Hudson found a dry patch beside the wall and sat down.

For some unaccountable reason he could not get Crawley out of his mind, although he knew there was little logic attached to his concerns. But why was Crawley in Scotland? It was a most unusual arrangement, and he could not remember another Galloway drove where a farm agent had travelled north, presumably to oversee aspects of the arrangements. Hudson usually arranged everything himself. He was used to it. And there had been no mention of any different arrangement in the offer letter he had received from Blakeney. Mr Porter had written merely that he needed the best man for this particular drove and that he, Hudson, was known in the locality, if not in the county as a whole, as the best man.

Hudson pondered the matter some more and then watched distractedly as a brogger with a small cart toiled up the hill beside the chapel. A woman and two small children trailed behind the waggon, and the man said, "Good day to ye," as he went by, absorbed in his task.

An hour later, as dusk began to settle around the hills, and after twice stopping to ask the way, Thomas Hudson finally trotted up the gravelled drive of The Lodge. He stopped momentarily by the gate when he first saw the house, and was surprised by its size. It stood in large grounds, solid and square and built of the local grey stone, with a sharply pitched roof and windows which, he guessed, overlooked some fine views. The front door was set in the centre of the four front windows, but before he could decide whether to ride to the front door or attend a more modest entrance to the rear, it was flung open. Light flooded out and two men came to greet him. Clearly, they had been watching for his arrival, and he saw immediately that one was Crawley. The other was a servant of some sort.

"My dear Mr Hudson," said Crawley, his angular features outlined by the candles inside. "May I welcome you to Durisdeer. My man will take your horse and bring in your bags. Please, refresh yourself in your own time. We will anxiously await your arrival in the drawing-room to hear the latest news of Norfolk, and to tell you of the floods, and then we shall have dinner. We have prepared a place for you."

Another surly servant carried his bags up the staircase and showed him to his room, which was much finer than he had slept in before and in which a fire had been lit so that he might dry his greatcoat. The manservant dumped the bags in the middle of the floor, without ceremony, and gave every indication of an insolent demeanour and a total lack of interest in his surroundings or the guests.

Before the man stumped out of the door Hudson asked, quite suddenly, "How long has Mr Crawley owned The Lodge?"

The man paused, and a passable look of contempt flickered across his face.

"Oh, Mr Crawley'll not own it, now or ever, God-willing. He has it for four weeks. That's all."

"He has rented it?"

"Aye, and paid good money, too, I'll be bound."

"Do you know him well?"

"No. Yon Sassenach arrived only three days' ago and brought his friends and the maid with him. A gentleman farmer from England, I'm told. That's all I know."

Then he was gone, clumping heavily down the stairs.

There were four men in the drawing-room when he finally entered, sipping whisky and sitting before a fireplace, and they all rose and turned towards him. Crawley introduced them as business partners and friends, but afterwards Hudson could not remember their names or what manner of business they professed to pursue. Nevertheless, Crawley was a charming host. When he rang for assistance, and a maid appeared, a glass of whisky for Hudson soon followed; and then another; and slowly Hudson began to feel at ease, the rough edges in his speech and mannerisms seemingly mattering less and less in such company. Indeed, Crawley's other guests also proved themselves men - despite their dress - of a world not dissimilar to Hudson's own, at times confident, and others raucous and vulgar. It was Crawley who was the one apart, being better educated than all of them, and even more at ease than they among the maids and servants, fine brocade furniture and crystal decanters.

Once or twice Hudson introduced the matter of the drove, but on each occasion Crawley pooh-poohed the subject, and the other guests looked away.

"Tomorrow," he said. "We shall do all the business tomorrow, and talk of it then."

A few minutes later the maid entered to announce dinner, and they rose unsteadily and walked into an adjoining room. The table was copious, the conversation cheerful and the drink freely available. Three hours later Hudson, more used to the rough ways of the drovers and sleeping at the roadside, slumped onto his strange, fine bed and fell into a befuddled, whisky-fuelled sleep.

Crawley was as good as his word. When, eventually, Hudson came downstairs the following morning it was to find a silent and apparently deserted house, with no sign of either of the servants or the maid. Nor did they seem to have been busy this morn, for the grate was uncleaned and as he passed the dining-room, and peered through the slightly open door, he could see the table had only partially been cleared. The debris of the previous evening's meal, including the bottles and glasses, was still there, littering the tablecloth. As for Crawley's cronies, Hudson presumed they were still abed.

For a while, and thoroughly curious, he amused himself by strolling through the quiet rooms, now filled with morning sunshine, looking at the furniture, fingering the materials and enjoying the sensuous pleasure of sights, smells and feelings he encountered only very rarely and which made him only more aware of his own rough, outdoor clothes and the comparative coarseness of his own upbringing. There were ornaments and trinkets and gilded chandeliers selected, he was sure, with great taste, paintings of people he did not know, and carpets of some foreign design and manufacture and so thick they displayed the imprint of his footsteps as he moved around. And outside, topiary and lawns and beds of flowers. Then, as he stood in the drawing-room looking from the window, and was on the point of considering a stroll in the garden, he heard a door close upstairs and the sound of someone descending to the ground floor. Crawley found him and beckoned him into yet another room which Hudson had not previously entered.

"I call it the library," Crawley said, half apologetically, closing the door behind him, "though I suppose it is more of a work room, for it is from here the estate is run."

There were books, it is true, and shelves lined with rolls and ledgers and deeds, but the small, tidy room was dominated by its desk and by two large chairs. Crawley finally seated himself at the desk and beckoned Hudson to be seated in the other chair some distance away. Then he took a bundle of papers from a drawer in the desk and began to look through them, leaving Hudson surrounded by silence and his own thoughts.

"Now, Hudson," he said. It was the first time Crawley had called him by his surname, and it seemed to reinforce the position of the one paying the wages. "It is time we talked of the matters in hand."

He seemed brisk and efficient and determined to control the conversation, and Hudson sensed a new authority about him. He wanted to ask Crawley why he had rented the house, and indeed, why he was in Scotland, but it did not seem the proper time.

"First," Crawley began, "my business friends have had to depart in order to reach Edinburgh as rapidly as possible. They left at dawn in order to gain a full day's ride. Regrettable, but true. In the event, and disappointed not to have seen you again after our convivial gathering last evening, they left their apologies and their kindest regards for a successful drove. It is a tiresome thing, business, for it works to no known clock."

Hudson shuffled uncomfortably on his chair and suddenly wished he was outside, in the garden.

"Be that as it may. You are licensed, I take it, with the papers in order?"

"Yes."

"Forgive my impertinence, but I must protect my employer's interests. And you will also be purchasing stock with some of your own bills of credit?"

"I will."

"Good. Now," Crawley continued, "the tryst is in three days' time, and I would expect you to leave for the south as soon as is practicable after that. We will attend the tryst together, of course, but in the meantime you are most welcome to stay here as my guest, and take your ease, and indeed, I insist that you do. There is also the unfortunate matter of the recent flooding. I have information, from friends who regularly travel considerable distances, that river levels are beginning to fall and the condition of the roads is improving. So once again, a few days of inaction should prove beneficial to all."

Hudson leaned forward in his chair, mildly irritated and determined to interject.

"Mr Crawley, I do not see how I can possibly idle away my time here for three days when you want to see a herd on the road south two or three days' after the tryst. I have a great deal to do. I have to examine and purchase cattle, put the drove together and arrange for them to be shod, hire hands, buy supplies. Deal with the banks. And to be frank I will depart when I am ready to depart, when I judge the roads ready, and when I judge we need to depart in order to be in Norfolk a good week before Fay's Fair. In the meantime, I have much work. I cannot enjoy the luxury of three days of idleness."

Crawley laid the papers back on his desk, tidied them, and then leaned back in his chair with his elbows on the chair arms, his fingers extended to support his long, aquiline chin. A clock in a corner of the room ticked loudly and mechanically.

"Let me begin again, Mr Hudson," he said quietly and deliberately, "in order to remove any further misunderstandings. You have contracted to take Mr Porter's drove to Norfolk. Yes? Correct? There is no contractual arrangement or obligation for you to carry liability for the entire herd."

The feelings of uncertainty and misgiving which had been with him ever since Crawley's note arrived at his lodging in Dumfries stirred once again in Hudson's mind, but all he could say was, "This is a most unusual arrangement. I do not fully understand it."

"Then let me be more specific. The herd will be in two parts. Mr Porter has entrusted me with certain financial arrangements relating to this drove.

In effect, he has entrusted me with considerable additional funding and the responsibility to purchase, with these additional funds, a proportion of the herd you will lead."

"What proportion?"

"Roughly thirty per cent. It is a most substantial investment, you will agree, and thanks to Mr Porter's foresight and generosity you will receive a generous remunerative advance to cover cues, stance money, the men's money, and your own fees. You are still responsible for purchasing the other seventy per cent - I believe you have made your financial arrangements for this - and for safeguarding the combined herd on its journey home."

"And you carry the risk for the thirty per cent?"

"Myself, I suppose. Myself, and of course, ultimately Mr Porter."

"And what size of combined herd?"

"About 600."

Hudson stared at him, perplexed. Alarmed. He had never come across this sort of combined drove before, with a land agent involved at this level.

"And where are your cattle?"

"They are selected and promised. They are on their way to the tryst."

"You have purchased them already?"

"Yes. And paid for them, on Mr Porter's behalf, though I have a few more details to settle with the bank, which I will do in two days' time. We will discuss the drivers' and topsman's pay later. I should add that Galloway prices are somewhat high at the moment, about five pounds and ten shillings, but they may reduce at the tryst when more herds arrive."

"But a herd that size . . . it will take many days to have them shod."

"I have already engaged a smith. He has been at work for two days."

"Engaging the services of a smiddy is my responsibility."

"For the cattle you secure, perhaps. But not for mine."

"And men. I shall need additional men."

"Again, you will find I have not been idle during my time here. I have already engaged some for the drove, on your behalf, including a topsman. You will meet them all at the tryst."

Hudson suddenly tensed, leaned forward and slammed his fists on the desk.

"I appoint my own topsman," he said sharply.

"There is no need, I assure you."

"I need someone I know and someone I can trust."

"My topsman is utterly trustworthy."

"No," he said.

"I beg your pardon?"

"I shall appoint my own topsman, and use my own men."

Quite suddenly Crawley's posture seemed to crumple, and he relaxed again. Finally he smiled and then gestured in the air with his hands.

"It is a small enough matter," he chortled dismissively. "We shall speak of it again and resolve these minor questions at the tryst. A minor matter. In the meantime the facilities of this house are available to you. You are most welcome to remain here safe in the knowledge that matters which seem to concern you have already been, and are being, resolved."

Thus, for Hudson, there began three days of enforced idleness during which he walked briskly and impatiently around the gardens to fill the emptiness, inspected the flower beds and the outbuildings and attempted discourse with a bent, wiry gardener whose dialect was so coarse they could scarce make each other understand, enjoyed his pipe, and mooned for hours around the house, looking at the paintings and running his fingers over the ornamental vases. Sometimes he thought of his wife, and of the prospect of the drove. But he saw little of Crawley, who seemed to be keeping out of his way, and choose not to converse with the surly, dissolute servants.

On the second day, and following a period of prolonged thought, he sat for a long time in his room composing and writing a letter to Mr Porter of Blakeney in which he expressed his surprise at the unusual nature of the arrangements, his own uncertainty regarding the style of the enterprise, and begged for some sort of reassurance. Perhaps Mr Porter might consider forwarding his reply to Bowes, where he would collect it on the way through? Later, on completion, he sealed the letter and handed it to the maid for presentation to the post runner and thence to one of the southern bound mail coaches.

On the third day there was delivered to the house a message from Isaac Swann confirming he had arrived at the tryst and that two more of the drivers had also arrived. But time still hung heavily, even though a weakling sun occasionally appeared and some of the floods began to recede.

The St Faith's drove trysting place was on about 200 acres of level ground surrounded on three sides by the bulky, rising outlines of the Lowther Hills, but the recent rains and the tramp of thousands of feet and hooves had changed its colour from summer green to dark winter brown. There were cattle as far as the eye could see, and the thunderous noise of lowing. The squealing, steaming black herds streamed across the flanks of the hillsides to the horizon on all sides, but underneath they wallowed in a morass of glutinous, oozing mud. It was a scene some would interpret as representative of hell itself: the thunderous lowing of the vast, seething herds, the nervous whinnying of horses and ponies and the yapping of drovers' dogs, the calling of men and beggars, and the racket and music of the sharpers and jesters, antics, fiddlers and ballard singers. They all contributed to the hubbub and the scenes of frantic activity and chaos which so horrified and perplexed anyone attending for the first time and thrilled those who knew the scene well. And knew the smells. Teeming, damp, unwashed humanity, in homespun tweeds and plaids and shoddy blankets, Sassenachs in greatcoats and porkpie hats, sheltering beneath tents and awnings, drinking heated whisky, cooking broth and mutton over open fires, counting and sorting cattle, heating pots of tar to mark individual cattle after sale, riggling and dealing and arguing, doing deals and shaking hands. Peat smoke, tar smoke and mire, whisky, heather, and waggonloads of muck and tad trampled in the mire. Tenterboys, thieves, smiths, ghillies, drovers, dealers, drivers, servants, bank clerks, tacksmen, apprentices, gentlemen, near-do-wells, tradesmen, topsmen and grimy women selling all manner of things.

It was a scene Hudson knew well and one that, despite the evident chaos, never failed to excite him. He pulled up the cob some distance away and looked across the seething trysting ground, and smiled and inhaled deeply, and then urged his mount forward and on into the heaving mass of men, mud and cattle. Crawley, he knew, was already there, probably among the bank booths, and it was not long before he saw in the distance the familiar face of Isaac Swann, who came across immediately. Hudson dismounted, his boots sinking into the mire, and the two men greeted each other afresh. Then Hudson told him of Crawley's proposals and his purchase of some of the cattle.

"I have already seen them," Swann said. "One of the Scottish dealers told me."

"What are they?"

Swann shrugged his shoulders unenthusiastically.

"A mixture of runts and a few stirks, mainly Galloway, and a small group of kyloes," he said. "I didn't look at their feet." His dejection was easy to recognise.

"I need to see them for myself," Hudson said. "Then I must make my own purchases, visit the bank, and find a smith."

"Most of Mr Crawley's herd are already shod. One of his men told me a smith with some apprentices to do the roping and throwing worked on them for several days, though not here. Mr Crawley must have paid them off. They also said some of the Highland herds have been delayed because of floods, but they should all be here by tomorrow."

Hudson nodded, adding defensively, "He's not my smith, you know. Crawley found him." Then he asked how many of his drivers had arrived.

"Three."

"We shall need them all, and more."

"There are more, with Mr Crawley's herd."

Swann evidently knew as much as he did, or as little.

"I'd better go and find Mr Crawley," Hudson said after Swann had indicated where he and the others would be waiting, not far from the Commercial Bank booth. He gathered the reins. Then as he mounted the cob he had an afterthought.

"Isaac," he called. "I'd like you to be topsman."

Swann looked up at him seated in the saddle.

"I heard tell you already had one."

Hudson shook his head. "If there is, he's not one of my men. Leave it to me. Will you do it?"

Isaac nodded, and then turned away to be swallowed up moments later by the bustling throng.

Thirty minutes later, after Hudson had threaded his way through the jostling throng and located Mr Crawley's herd on the far side of the trysting ground, a swift glance told him that Swann's assessment seemed accurate. They were indeed a moderate lot, and some of the stirks looked a mite too young and frail. Nevertheless, they seemed to have been shod.

He tied the cob to a post holding a line of fleaks, opened a narrow gap in a section of the wattle hurdles wide enough for him to squeeze through, and pushed and slapped his way into the middle of the uneasy, restive herd. Without any roping he looked at their hooves as best as he could. The cues seemed to have been nailed properly, outside clove only, four to an animal. He preferred eight, but it was a costly business and, fortuitiously, the ground was likely to be soft. Then he did a swift calculation. Assuming this was the sum total of Crawley's cattle, then he estimated between 250 and 300 head, perhaps a few more, all of them with Crawley's mark and all apparently shod. They represented an enormous aditional investment to that which Mr Porter had already allowed him, and he wondered why Mr Porter had done the business like this. Again, a smiddy and two or three helpers to make the nails, do the roping and the throwing, shoe the outers only, and working from dusk until dawn, could do about 70 a day. So there was five or six days' work here, and more for the marking, which meant they must have begun the task well before the tryst and driven them to the ground already shod.

For some reason he felt a keen sense of disappointment. It was as though Crawley was controlling events, dictating things, even attempting to leave him sidelined, and it was not a feeling he had encountered before.

Hudson pushed his way out of the herd and scrambled back through the fleaks, and was pushing the hurdle into place beside the post when he became aware of two drovers bearing down on him. They were large, unyeilding, unfriendly, begrimed Scots, plaids folded across their chests, carrying large poles and reeking of smoke and heather, which meant they had been sleeping in the open. They positioned themselves threateningly on either side of him.

"You'll not be goin' without telling us who y'are," one of them said. He was of considerable stature, wide-shouldered, and older than his companion who seemed to walk in his awe.

"My name is Thomas Hudson, drove master from Norfolk. I am in charge of Mr Crawley's herd. This is Mr Crawley's herd, is it not?"

"Aye, but what are you doin' inspectin' them?"

"They are my responsibility. I presume, if you have been engaged by Mr Crawley and are in his employ, that it is your responsibility to assist me to look after them."

"We know our responsibilities, Englishman."

"Good. Then I shall have to make sure you carry them out, because in future, if you want to be paid you will have to make sure you also do as you're told."

"We'll tell topsman you have arrived," said the large one.

"I have my own topsman."

"Mr Crawley has already told Andrew he has the job."

"Then you can tell Andrew, whoever he is, that he has just lost the job. If he wants to join the drove he can. If he does not, then Mr Crawley will pay him off."

"Andrew will not like it, and nor will we," said the tall one.

Hudson looked him full in the eyes.

"In that case it is extremely unlikely that any of you will be paid," he said quietly. Then he untied the reins of his cob, slipped into the saddle, and rode off to find the rest of his men. Behind him, the two Scots drovers glowered after his receding outline. When he disappeared they finally slopped away through the mud.

Hudson was greatly troubled by the events of the day, and scarce knew what to make of them, but he went through the motions of preparation, as he had done so many times before on so many other droves, and occupied his mind as best he could. Only once did he see Crawley, late in the day, as Crawley was evidently preparing to return to the house for the night. They spoke briefly and civilly to each other, but this time Hudson declined to return with him, preferring to stay overnight at the tryst with his men. The matter settled, the two men agreed to separate and meet and talk again on the morrow.

Hudson drove himself relentlessly, while the light lasted and while the drovers and dealers were still sober enough to do business. He engaged a smith - whom he knew from previous travels - and his handlers and apprentices, to make the nails, and then presented his Promissory Notes at the British Linen Bank booth. The bankers knew him and, business done and papers signed, the Notes of Credit were soon forthcoming. Then he found Swann and his three regular men, gave the trio money and sent them to purchase supplies of food, and spare leather and iron cues, and told Swann to engage three additional men willing to go south. Only when this was done did he begin the painstaking task of buying cattle to add to the drove.

By nightfall, and despite much riggling and arguing, he was still a hundred head short, so he ate with the men and then, wrapped in his greatcoat, slept fitfully, continually disturbed by the noise of drunken revels elsewhere on the trysting ground. Fortunately the night was cloudy and fine, and the herds were quiet, and in the morning he began work again.

Crawley sought him out early, as soon as there was some heat in the sun. Hudson was talking to a dealer when Crawley rode up and beckoned him across. The visitor did not dismount, but stayed mounted, and looked down on his man with a degree of superiority.

"Hudson, I have had Andrew to see me, and the other men. They are not happy."

"I did not anticipate they would be."

"I had already appointed Andrew as topsman, and I expect him to fulfill that role."

"And I relieved him of the role. As I told you at the house, I have my own topsman."

"You have never met Andrew. He is a good man and I want you to reinstate him."

"No, sir. I will not. Isaac Swann is my topsman, agreed and appointed."

"What if I insist?"

"Then, sir, you can find yourself another master ready to leave at very short notice."

Crawley stared at him for a moment with anger etched across his face, but he said merely, "Very well," pulled and reins sharply and turned away.

Later that night, by the light of Swann's fire, Hudson wrote up the day's events in his journal, did the accounts and worked out his final tally. The tally read:

"Black Galloway runts, 531; Ayrshires, 20; kyloes, 22; polled Angus, 14; stirks, 14; Pembroke oxes, 8; total, 609. Myself, master, and Isaac Swann, topsman. My men, Richard Kerridge, Jeremiah Thurston and his collie, William Venning. Mr Crawley's men, Andrew, John Bell, Hugh Faichney. Swann's men, Macculloch, Charles Pearse, Tillyard."

His monetary calculations were less circumspect. He had to pay the men's wages, purchase the supplies, and pay the smiths, the tolls, the stance money and the finishing reward. Experience told him it would also cost at least £1 3s a head to get the herd to St Faith's. Then there might be additional losses of over £1 a head in terms of body weight loss, or through rinderpest, accident or over-driving. Add to that the purchase cost, subtract the cash Crawley had already given him, and he realised he would need some buoyant selling prices in Norfolk. That night Hudson fell asleep telling himself he would have to be very careful if he was to break even.

Six days' later, the shoeing and preparations complete, Hudson's drove - one of a number of herds crawling slowly over the landscape at that particular time of the year - reached the northern outskirts of Dumfries, where he halted them for the night. Then he decided to divide the restive herd into smaller groups and began moving them again at first light the following morning. The drivers with their sticks, apparently oblivious to the ceaseless cacophony of noise, walked alongside or sensibly let their mounts do their work, which they did instinctively. The homing sense of the herd was still strong, which made it sluggish and fractious, but it had been a reasonable two-day journey from the trysting ground. Temperate weather, meaning there had been no further rain, dictated that stream levels were beginning to fall and the sodden ground was starting to dry out. Save for one or two problems it had all gone reasonably well.

One setback they encountered was that young Faichney, one of Crawley's three hired Scots, was nowhere to be found, which caused Hudson to ponder the possibility of a replacement until John Bell, who seemed to have lost much of his aggressive attitude since the tryst, confessed he had seen Faichney ride off towards Dumfries, presumably for the drink, and that they would probably pick him up as they streamed through the town. Fortunately, it happened that Swann was still with the group, and he helped out until it was time for him to reconnoitre the town and find an overnight stance, which was not easy or cheap now that the herd was so large and White Sands still under water. So the herd moved away from the Lowther Hills like a black river, or even a giant snake, crawling over the undulating landscape, ebbing and flowing, bulging and thinning, twisting and contorting. A second problem was related to the two bright, moonlight nights encountered on the way to Dumfries, which made the fretful herd restless and homesick and inclined to wander, so that there was little sleep for any of the men or their ponies. Only Thurston's collie somehow retained its enthusiasm and boundless energy.

On the day they left the trysting ground Hudson also had his first encounter with Crawley's third hiring, Andrew, to whom John Bell and young Faichney seemed to defer with some awe. Andrew turned out to be a soft-spoken Scot, muscular and broad shouldered, who walked with a slight limp and yet who had an undisguised air of authority about him. The two greeted each other civilly, as two equals on common ground, and slowly explored their relationship. In answer to Hudson's questioning, no, Andrew was not resentful of losing the job of topsman, even though Crawley had given it to him; and yes, he needed the work. He also needed an opportunity to spend time in England, and perhaps stay longer to find work there, for there was precious little, he said, in Scotland. He had been a drover for some years. Before that he had been with Wellington in Portugal and had fought at Vittoria, which was a famous battle everyone had heard of because they pushed the French back into their own country, and at the crossing of the Nivelle river, which no one had heard of and where he had taken a piece of Frenchie lead shot in his thigh. He had returned home after several years wounded and penniless to find his sole parent, his father, dead, and the family cot demolished to make room for new sheep ranges. Since then he had been moving around Scotland doing various jobs and never settling anywhere.   Hudson recalled hearing that in the 1790s the Pembroke Militia were billeted at Holt during the time of the French invasion scare, but otherwise he knew little of military matters. However, hearing his story, and concluding that he was probably a brave man, Hudson decided that he could probably like him if he could learn to trust him, for they seemed to have matters in common. One example was that Andrew could evidently read and write. Yet Hudson retained in his mind the fact that Andrew was a Crawley hiring, and Crawley's first choice as topsman. It created a tiny cloud of suspicion which he felt would take a long time to disperse.

Swann rode back to the stance while it was still dark and found Hudson motionless on his cob on one of the flanks of the herd. The first thin fingers of light were threatening to appear in the sky, and Hudson kept flexing his fingers to banish the tentacles of cold.

"The waters are dropping, but White Sands is still flooded," Swann whispered, not wishing to disturb the stock. "The town is quiet. Go straight through. I would start now, before the streets are busy."

Hudson nodded. "Where is tonight's stance?"

"Cummertrees."

He nodded again. He knew the place.

"And have you seen the young Scot?"

This time it was Swann's time to nod his head.

"Yes, I have seen him. He was thrown out of the Globe last night, for some unpleasantness or other, and the last I saw of him he was sleeping on the steps of the Queensberry column. The herd will catch up with him."

And so they did. Two hours later the black river poured through the deserted, sleeping streets of the town and out the other side, waking the befuddled Faichney as the stream of beasts parted and poured past him on either side of the monument where he had spent much of the night. The cacophony of lowing and the constant rattle and racket of shod hooves on stone coggles also woke everyone else and caused candles and lamps to be lit, and doors to swing open and hurridly close again. An hour later, and by the time the last of the animals had clattered clear of the town, with John Bell in their wake ambling beside his pony, the final vestiges of night had gone and the main streets of Dumfries were covered in a carpet of stinking tad.

Slowly, deliberately, the drove made its way towards bleak and misty Bankend where the road was exposed and a sharp wind whipped off the Solway Firth, causing the men to pull their plaids and greatcoats even tighter around their shoulders, and then they turned towards Cummertrees. The herd's movement was slow, but Hudson noted with satisfaction that Andrew, Bell, Thurston and Venning, and the three men Swann had hired, all knew the job well and worked willingly and easily, and without being told, though he was less sure about the drunken youngster, Hugh Faichney, or about Richard Kerridge, another young lad, from Norfolk, who seemed preoccupied and lost in thought most of the time.

Later, when the light was leaving the sky and glinting a farewell on the distant Firth, they found the stance among the gentle hills and settled the herd, and Hudson, Kerridge, Pearse and Tillyard sat around a small fire which Charles Pearse had lit and over which they had been mixing crowdie, cooking bannocks and slices of onion on a hot stone, and warming the whisky. It was becoming increasingly cold as the night deepened, and they would all be glad to be away from the edge of the water.

"You'll be taking us over the Firth, Mr Hudson?" Tillyard asked. "There's Dornock Wath and Stoney Wath to come, so we could make Bowness in good time."

"No, I shall not," Hudson said. "Too many have been lost in the trying, and I do not think the taking of the risk would altogether please our topsman."

They all laughed and leaned forward towards the fire for warmth.

They knew it was possible to cross the Firth, to avoid the Gretna toll and reduce the time to England, and many drovers and herds had done it. But it required tide, wind, moonlight, timing and the condition of the sands all in precise balance, otherwise it was a treacherous endeavour. Indeed, they all knew the story, oft repeated over the years, of drover George Moore who halted his herd on the shore opposite Boulmer and waited for low tide. Then when low tide came he waited for moonlight, and when they did finally set off for the far shore he had left it too late. The tide was turning, the wind had changed, and a few miles from shore the water rose and swirled around their barrels. Although the men and their ponies were able to scramble to safety the cattle had to swim for it, and many were swept away. It had happened since and it would happen again.

"The Firth is a dangerous illusion," Hudson said.

So they chided the miserable Kerridge instead. He had been sitting by the fire, head down, draped in a tattered greatcoat, rocking back and forth and staring at the flames. And he had said nothing.

"You'll not make a good driver while you remain in such bad humour," Pearse said. "You'll make the herd miserable, too."

"I'll smile when the mood takes me," Kerridge mumbled. "And not until."

"What you need is a good woman," Pearse went on. "An eligible widow with four or five bastards, each one bringing in the relief. Then you can marry her and live off the income."

Kerridge, who had seen barely fifteen summers and who had spent most of those away from home, shuffled uncomfortably and was beginning to show signs of agitation.

"Leave the boy alone," said Hudson at last, and Pearse and Tillyard finally went about their business.

Soon after Kerridge struggled to his feet, glancing at Hudson as he did so, as though in thanks, and shuffled away to find a corner in which to sleep until one of the others woke him during the small hours for his turn to help look after the herd.

That night Hudson wrote in his journal: "Cummertrees, and three days done. Losses: nought."

Because of the bad conditions likely to be encountered on the way, and the likelihood of crowded roads, Hudson had already decided to avoid Carlisle, Penrith and Eamont Bridge, which was the usual route, and follow the Eden river instead. And by the time the Gretna toll was behind them, Carlisle was to the west, and the herd was beginning to pick its careful way towards the valley of the Eden river, beast and man were starting to settle into the routine of the drove. This inevitably involved an early start followed by a stop when the sun was high, and sometimes a second halt if the way had been hard and Hudson thought they were tiring. Then a long afternoon and a late evening until the night stance - which Swann would have found and hired - was reached. The cattle grazed as they rested, and drank from the streams, but the men and their ponies, and Thurston's collie, were not so fortunate. They were constantly alert, listening and watching, and always tired. They ate and refreshed themselves when they could, mostly at the stance, sometimes in the open and occasionally, if there was an inn nearby, inside. It was a monotonous existence. Water and whisky and ale, if there was an inn, bannock, crowdie, brose or oatmeal if they were outside, and sometimes gruel, beef or mutton and onions if they could persuade a landlord to let them take over a parlour and luxuriate, and steam, at a table in front of an open fire. All of them slept in the open rolled in their plaids or greatcoats, whatever the weather, and they worked in shifts so that three or four of them were always out noiselessly patrolling the boundaries of the herd, keeping things quiet, coaxing the beasts back if any were tempted to stray, keeping an eye open for thieves or predators or anything that might cause a feeling of fear to run like wildfire through the massed black ranks.

With Gretna behind them Hudson and the cob also began to relax. To begin with, his mind was full of Jenny, the mare he had been forced to sell to the Moorend knacker, and it was not until they were in the open countryside again that he realised the feeling of loss was properly behind him. A mount was a mount, and now he had another good one. Jenny, he decided, represented a part of his life which was gone. Also, the town was full of sharpers and dealers, toffs and chaises, waggons and carts, and the size of the herd, and the time it took them to bypass the town, won them no friends. The drivers of carts which had to pull over and wait, and knots of people stranded in their doorways by the ever flowing stream of jostling beasts, shook their fists and swore at them as they went by. He was also worried at the prospect, in such narrrow streets, of two or three of the animals being cut from the herd without their knowledge and hidden in barns and stores and back gardens until they had passed on. It was the custom after a count that the day's losses were reported to him. But no one came.

Despite splashing through innumerable streamlets or paddling through a sea of mud, it was not until they reached the Eden bridge that they really began to run into difficulties again. The bridge was stone and well built, but in the centre it funnelled, like the neck of a bottle, and it had always been difficult with a large herd. Somehow you had to squeeze the leading beasts through the neck, which slowed them down, and at the same time prevent the great mass of the herd, which was behind them, from trampling forward too soon and from panicking when they found they could not make progress. However, Hudson was ready for this. Long before they reached the bridge he told his men to slow the herd down almost to a standstill and then to divide it into smaller groups, so that the groups might make transit over the wide river one cluster at a time. There was the added problem, too of increasing traffic on the road, moving north from England, or travelling south along the old Roman road towards the Stainmoor Pass, and soon the roads on either side of the bridge became jammed with shiny, expensive horses, gentlemen riders wearing stiff collars, cravats and black, long-tailed coats, restless teams and coaches full of irate passengers, loaded waggons pulled by cowed and exhausted creatures, and even a jagger with a train of 20 pack ponies carrying Scottish woollen garments and goodness knows what else into the south. What concerned Hudson even more, there were also several knots of hangers-on and near-do-wells idling about and evidently enjoying the noise and chaos.

Once the first elements of the herd began to seep across the bridge Hudson's team was kept in a ferment of action, for the animals already over the river had to be halted and quietened, the coaches and road traffic allowed its chance to cross, and then the later elements of the herd kept in check and prevented from straying or becoming too restless. His concern was not idle fussing, for they all knew of the disaster some years earlier when a herd walking south from Dumfries, in going over the bridge, had met a mail coach coming in the opposite direction. The herd had panicked, the bridge parapet had given way under the pressure of dozens of bodies, and animals and men had been ejected to their deaths into the river below. The authorities had been forced to rebuild the bridge.

So there were many moments of genuine tension, and Hudson's humour was not helped when he saw four of the near-do-wells in earnest conversation with Andrew, holding his pony's bridle, near the far side of the bridge. He watched them for as long as he could, and at last he saw Andrew rein away and rejoin the others on the perimeter of the herd, while the wretched foursome laughed and talked among themselves as they wandered off. Three hours later they were all across the river, thanks to some tireless work by the men and by Thurston's collie, but somewhere in the melee two beasts were lost and there was no time to search for them. Later, in his blackest moments, Hudson wondered if they had been deliberately cut out unnoticed in the chaos at the bridge.

The Eden valley way by Broadwath to Armathwaite was pleasant enough, the road gliding through a gently wooded landscape of occasional miserable villages fringed on both sides by the distant hills. Nearer Armathwaite the valley narrowed and the road started to climb, so Hudson moved the herd towards the slightly easier ground to the east, close to the river, and halted them before they began to tackle the rise towards Lazonby.

At one rest halt late in the day, when everything was quiet and the horses were drinking, Andrew rode up to Hudson. He obviously wanted to talk, and seemed troubled.

"I may have to leave the drove," he said, matter-of-factly.

"Why would that be? I would not like it to happen."

Andrew fiddled with the buckle of a girth, uncertain how to continue. Then he said:

"You saw the men speak to me at the bridge?

Hudson nodded, for the incident had not been far from his mind for two days.

"I know these men. They are unpleasant companions, but unfortunately they have a hold on me. I owe them money, and I do not have the ability to pay."

"And?"

"They are threatening to cut beasts from the herd if I do not pay. Therefore, it would be better if I left. It is the only thing left for me to do. At least they might chase after me, and it would draw them away from you."

Hudson thought for a moment. He had seen the men, and wondered about them, but at least he was no longer nervous of Andrew's loyalty.

"If you did depart," he asked, "is there any certainty they would leave the the herd alone?"

"No."

"That is honest."

"I mean, there is no certainty. Aye, they would pursue me, but there is no certainty."

"What is the money?"

"It goes back to a time when I was in Edinburgh, when I was foolish. I could not pay it back them and I cannot pay now, but they know my work and in what part of the country I usually work, and so I cannot be rid of them."

"What does the sum amount to?"

"Twenty pounds. They have a note which I signed."

"And would they leave you and the herd alone if it was paid?"

"Yes, I think so. But it is a great deal of money, far beyond my means."

Hudson weighed his options, once against the other, and then asked the question uppermost in his mind.

"Is this the work of Mr Crawley?"

Andrew looked askance, and weighed his words before he answered.

"No, not exactly. All this happened a long time before I met Crawley."

"So are you still Crawley's man?"

Once again Andrew hesitated.

"I have no love for Crawley. He is a clever and devious man. He knew I was in debt, so he asked if I would join your drove as topsman, and that you would pay me if I did. He also said that if I helped to prevent the herd reaching Norfolk he would pay me a considerable bonus which would enable me to pay off my debt. I no longer wish to claim the bonus, or harm the herd. Quite the contrary. Which is why I think I should leave, to draw my creditors away from you."

Hudson was still puzzled.

"Why should Crawley not want the herd to reach Norfolk? Of what possible advantage to him would such a situation be?"

"I do not know, but I do know the scheme also involves some of his cronies, and some land somewhere."

Land?

"What land?"

"I do not know."

"And what of Bell and Faichney? Are they still Crawley's men?"

"No. They are my men, though they know of Crawley's offer."

"Will they carry through the plan to stop the herd?"

"Not if I tell them not to. They are good men, but they are also very poor, and it is hard for them to earn a wee crumb for their families."

Hudson allowed the cob to drink its fill, and then pulled its head away from the water, making up his mind as he did so. He drew in his breath, aware of the risk he was about to take.

"If I gave you twenty pounds would you go to find your creditors and pay them off? And would you return?"

Andrew looked at him in surprise, and then nodded.

"Aye, I would. And gratefully."

"Then that is what we will do. I will trust you. I will give you the credit notes to pay off the debt, and allow you to ride off. If I am right about you then you will do the necessary business and return to the drove. If I am wrong, I shall lose twenty pounds and a good herder."

Andrew looked at him thoughtfully.

"But how would I repay you?"

"We will discuss the matter later, but there will be no need to sign papers. It will suffice if we can discuss the matter as friends."

"Thank you. I thought all Englishmen were like Mr Crawley. Now I see they are not."

Some time later Hudson gave Andrew the credit notes and watched him ride away, believing in his heart he would never see either again. But he was wrong. The herd ambled on towards Lazonby and the high ground beyond, and the day dragged monotonously, but finally Andrew was back, and before they reached Culgaith.

"It is done?" Hudson asked when he rode close to him.

"It is done," said Andrew, smiling. "I found them at an inn, and paid them. They gave me the paper. It is done, and they are drinking themselves into a stupour."

Now the countryside was becoming wilder and more remote, and the inclines steeper. Clumps of broom and gorse mottled the heathland and outcrops of rock and piles of stones dotted the slopes, and the herd seemed to trail over several miles of hilly landscape. Then one day, traipsing the Roman road shortly before Brough - the place of the famous fair - appeared on the horizon, Macculloch, who had been bringing up the rear, told him some of the stirks were tiring and a few others were limping. Thurston, too, said he had noticed one with blood on his hooves, but at the time he had not been able to take a close look.

Hudson, worried and suspicious, had already noticed the deterioration and had instantly decided upon a course of action. First, he would order a tally, setting one of the drivers to count the sections of the herd as they moved by, which he did with the old method, "yan, tan, tethera," and so on, in a long, sonorous, monotonous chant. Second, he decided to consider matters further at Brough, even though he had no love for the place and had no wish to stay.

In his journal that night he wrote: "At Brough. Nine days gone. Total losses thus far, 2, meaning the herd now 607."

Thomas Hudson spent a fretful , cold night wrapped in his greatcoat, lying on damp grass with one shoulder hard against a clump of wet rock, his mind listening to the sighing and shuffling of the herd and an occasional cough from one of his men as they patrolled the boundaries, silent as the grave so as not to disturb the runts. Fortunately the night was overcast and there were no stars, so the tired animals were content to graze and rest. And so, by and large, were the men. Faichney was different, though. As soon as the herd was settled and Andrew told the youngster to take rest and eat, Faichney collected his pony, ostensibly to purchase oatmeal, and slipped into Brough, a short distance over the rise. A miserable enough place at the best of times, it did nevertheless boast the Golden Fleece and two or three bush houses, and it was not long before jugs of ale rotted his memory and his control. Faichney forgot all about the supplies, which was a pity because the inns were invariably well stocked for just such an occasion as a herd coming through. Instead, and long after dark, Andrew found him insensible in the street, his pony wandering free and a group of local sheep men and labourers, equally inebriated, about to play on him some prank which no doubt would have left him even worse for wear. Andrew brushed them aside, cajoled someone to catch Faichney's pony and somehow managed to lay him across its back, his unconcious young head lolling and rolling in tune to the movement of the creature, and brought him back to the herd where they washed his face in stream water, wrapped him in coats, and laid him down to sleep.

"He has this terrible craving," Andrew said when Hudson went to hear the news. "I fear for him sometimes. He is so young."

The problem of how to re-invigorate the herd also exercised Hudson's mind during the long hours of the night. Some of Crawley's beasts were already showing signs of tiredness, the stirks were exhausted, and even though they had not left their ponies for closer inspections, the men reported having seen a total of seven with blood around their hooves. It was worrying news in such wet weather, when gangrene could so easily set in, and with some hard roads to come, but they would have to wait for daylight to rope and throw a sample to look at their feet. On the other hand, if he wanted to cross Stainmoor Pass and make Bowes in a day they would need to be off long before dawn.

In a sense the matter was resolved for him. He was awakened from a light sleep by Tillyard who said a passing carter had brought a message from Swann to the effect that he had secured a cheap stance at Bowes, only a shout from the old castle. A farmer, plied with drink by a group of his friends had agreed, in front of them all, a rental of only sixpence a score, a third of the usual price, and this at a time when the price of grazing was rising. Swann knew several of the farmer's equally drunken friends, and they would back up the agreement. Hudson knew it was too good an opportunity to miss. The herd was tired, but they would rise early, cross the Pass in a day, and rest there awhile should it become necessary.

Long before the first wisps of morning light showed in the eastern sky the clamourous herd was on the move, winding slowly through sleeping South Stainmoor and then on up the slopes of Moudy Mea. The ground was wet and slippery, rugged and desolate, and pitted with rocky outcrops, and there were uncomfortable numbers of streams and rivulets to be waded. In addition the new day, when it came, was overcast and autumn mists hung like curtains around the hills, and it was not long before a mixture of perspiration and drizzle was trickling down their faces and chilling their bodies. The backs of the horses and the cattle shone with moisture and sweat, and even Thurston's uppity collie seemed to have lost weight, its coat clinging so tightly to its seemingly inexhaustible body.

For four hours they toiled up the slopes and among the rocks, slipping and sliding and cursing, and then on a plateau Hudson called a brief halt. The riders relaxed, the herd, shuffled and sidled and then stopped, perplexed, and all around them the mist hung in a grey drape so that they could not tell how far they had been or how far they had to go.

Thurston rode up to Hudson.

"I do not like the way things are," the old drover said. "Some of the runts are exhausted and some are bleeding about the hoof. They need rest and re-shoeing."

"I do not understand why they are so affected, except that Crawley engaged his own smith," said Hudson. "But yes, I know they are tired. We will rest the herd at Bowes and consider things there."

"Some of them may not make Bowes," Thurston said bluntly. "They are exhausted."

"I know, but there is no grazing here. The grass is too short and sparse, and the weather can be bad. We must go on."

So they went on, slipping and sliding over the rocks and the wet grass, slithering down the inclines and toiling up the slopes, and all the time mists tried to conceal their endeavours. Once, sometime around midday, one of the Ayrshires slipped and tumbled over an ankle-high outcrop, and roared in pain, and Pearse saw immediately it had broken a leg. He dismounted, took a knife from his belt, and slaughtered it quietly so as not to alarm the rest of the herd. Then he and Macculloch worked frantically to butcher it and cut small pieces of some of the best meat to feed the collie and cook for themselves over the fires, or to have cooked at some nearby inn. The rest of the carcase, the majority of it, they left. From afar, it looked like a black and red marker on the grey hillside.

By the time they came off Moudy Mea and reached Hard Hills the long writhing snake of the herd, and the horses, were tiring visibly, and they lost more animals when a pair of awkward runts took it into their heads to elude Macculloch and wander off into the mist. Macculloch rode after them, as far as he dare without losing visual contact with the herd, but he could not see or hear them, and eventually gave up the chase. And a short distance further on a young stirk, stricken with exhaustion, slowly subsided on to its knees, and despite the efforts and encouragement of Thurston and Venning it was clearly unable to move. Pearse came and slaughtered it, too. Then late in the day, beyond Hard Hills on the fringes of Bowes Moor, the ground at last started to fall away in front of them in a series of gentle slopes, and they began to leave the desolation behind them.

They reached Bowes in the evening, the herd lame and exhausted, the men tired and hungry and wet, and Hudson saw immediately the grazing was good. Swann had left a message with the disgruntled but not unwilling farmer to say they could stay for up to four days, should they need to do so, and before the next herd was due. Hudson's first concern was the condition of the animals, and he gathered all the men and bid them go into the herd and inspect them, and asked Kerridge, Thurston and Venning to rope and throw some of the runts with blood on their legs and look at their cloves. Then with the herd quiet and settled, and well grazed, and leaving the three Scots in charge, the rest of the men withdrew to the ruins of the old castle and set up temporary camp. Venning soon had a fire going, and

Galloway beef and onions cooking, and moistened oatmeal and whisky warming, and they ate heartily and dried themselves as best they could.

A little later Andrew rode up, his pony's hooves clattering on the stone floor of the old castle, and he came over and squatted beside Hudson and the others, warming himself by the fire.

"One wee stirk had convulsions, and so I butchered it, and the others need at least two days' rest," he said.

Hudson nodded. He was already resigned to losing time here.

"There is more," Andrew said soberly, so that they all knew something was wrong, and looked at him in anticipation. "We have been doing some roping and looking at the cloves, and some of them are bleeding badly. A few have cues that are loose and several have some missing. They will need renailing."

They looked at each other, the light from the fire flickering across their faces.

"Why is this?" Hudson asked at last, unhappy at the thought of losing even more time.

Andrew opened his clenched fist to display a selection of cue nails, some of them bent and twisted. Hudson picked one up and examined it.

"What does this mean?"

"It means someone made the wrong nails. They should be one and one-eighth inches. These are half an inch. They have a good flat head, but they are too short," he said.

Hudson's expression changed to one of consternation. Now he was angry and perplexed.

"At the tryst," he said, "I examined Crawley's herd and looked at their feet, and they seemed to have been nailed properly. I do not understand how I missed this."

Andrew explained, "You would have missed it very easily. The heads are made the usual size, so that when they are hammered in they look as though they have been done properly. It is only when you pull one out and look at it that you can see they are too short. These nails have been made too short, but made to look properly done."

"Then we must re-nail."

"We only have a few spare cues and scarcely no nails."

"Then we must have more made here in Bowes, and we must stay until they are done and until the runts are rested."

The rest of the men agreed. The herd could not journey much further until they did.

The note in Hudson's journal, written that night shortly before riding off to take his turn with the herd, was suitably brief: "Ten days gone, and a delay. Losses, 7. Herd, 602."

Slowly a deeper, more ingrained and relaxing sort of routine was emerging now that the herd had lost its homing instinct. By day the men shared the tasks and the watches, and caught up on their sleep, and by night those not on watch huddled in the recesses of the crumbling stone walls and took what ease they could. The old castle stood square and tall, roofless and ruinous, but it offered some shelter from the wind and sometimes, when it rained, they could find protection by squeezing into the old doorways and alcoves, or on to the open staircase. The central square portion of the castle, already a tangle of weeds and grasses, quickly became potmarked and glutinous with the marks of old fires and debris and the endless tramp of ponies and people. But it proved a useful watch place, because through the gaping arches they could see the black mass of the herd lower down the valley, which the Romans knew, and hear the never ending, reassuring lowing of the cattle.

In the morning Hudson entrusted Andrew and Venning with sufficient coins and instructed them to engage a smith to make new nails and extra cues and, with the smiddy's apprentices, and also helped by Tillyard and Pearse, to begin the task of throwing, roping and re-shoeing. By noon they had begun, and the smith was with the herd, and those resting at the castle could see smoke from the smith's fires drifting across the valley, and pinpoints of flame twinkling in the gloom. Then Swann, droplets of moisture glistening on his beard, arrived to help out, having heard of the delay from one of a number of travellers he had come across waiting beside an overturned coach for a hastily summoned chaise from Bowes to retrieve them and return them to town. One set of coach wheels had evidently sunk into soft ground on the downward slope of a hill. The whip had hastily applying the skid, they told him, but to no avail. Thankfully, though, no-one had been hurt. Swann also brought news of another herd up ahead, already approaching Catterick.

"I believe it is Tait from Homersfield. He has about four hundred."

"And there are more herds behind us. How is the grazing?"

Swann seemed little concerned.

"There is enough. The rain came at the right time in England, and there was less of it, so it is much better than in Scotland. Tait usually turns towards Huntingdon, anyway," he said. It was some consolation.

"We need good quality grass for these creatures, for they are a poor lot."

Swann nodded.

"You will get it," he said.

Hudson was not reassured, but at least he knew Swann would do his best.

Afterwards, and feeling dejected and anxious, and having ascertained to his further chagrin that there was no letter for him in town from Mr Porter of Blakeney, Hudson promptly rode off to the herd to join the shoeing. Once again his fears began to crowd in upon him. He could not understand why Mr Porter had evidently not written, and even began to wonder if Crawley had somehow intercepted his original letter. But his thoughts were soon crowded out by the business of the day.

It was some time towards dusk that Hudson found himself alone in the castle ruins with the raggedly dressed and still morose Kerridge, the lad of fifteen summers, and he determined to speak to him there and then.

Kerridge was minding the fire in a corner by the castle wall, where earlier they had heated the broth, and he was poking it idly with a stick, sending showers of sparks flying into the air, watching the flames with dead, unblinking eyes. Hudson sat beside him.

"Where is your family?" he asked at length.

"I have none," said the boy, flatly and quite unemotionally.

"You mean you never knew them?"

"I remember them, but they are no more."

"How is that?"

Kerridge shrugged his shoulders and stared at the flames.

"I think a Wymondham farmer did for my father, for stealing meat," he mumbled. "They said the farmer's bailiff discovered the loss of a sheep. There was much snow on the field, and spots of blood, and the marks of three or four men and a laden donkey. Later, the bailiff dug up the skin of a butchered sheep, and three men, including my father, were sent to the Quarter Sessions. They were sentenced to the hulks, followed by the transports."

"What happened then?"

"He was chained in a hulk at Deptford for a long time and then taken to Portsmouth. Later on he was sent to New South Wales on the frigate Chas Kerr. That is all I know."

"And your mother?"

He shrugged his shoulders again.

"She disappeared. Went away."

"And left you?"

This time Kerridge said nothing, but bent his head and concentrated on peeling pieces of bark off the stick with a finger-nail.

"You have no brothers or sisters?"

"No, none."

"How long ago was this?"

Kerridge shrugged his shoulders again.

"I cannot remember. Three or four winters."

"And you have been on your own all this time?"

"In summer I work the droves and in winter I go to Norwich and get food where I can. Sometimes I work the stables. Stables and horses are warm."

"Do you ever think of your father?"

He stirred the fire again, and sparks leapt into the air.

"Not now. He has gone to another life, which is better than finishing one on the end of a rope."

"And you. What do you want to do?"

"Go to America," said Kerridge, lifting his eyes momentarily. "I do not think there will ever be anything for me here."

Then he lapsed into silence again, and Hudson left him alone with his sadness and the flames.

On the second day, when there was still no word from Mr Porter, Andrew told Hudson the herd had been checked as best they could and they had found eleven with badly bleeding feet where the nails had come free and the cues had dropped off. Hudson immediately decided to cut his losses, so they took them from the herd and sold them at the Bowes' flesh market at a time when the rowdy town was full of traders and smiths, dealers, and self importance. On the second day, too, Faichney drank himself insensible at the crowded Ancient Unicorn, only to be savagely kicked awake by Macculloch. They also perceived increased amounts of traffic coming through Bowes heading west towards Stainmoor and Carlisle, and then Galloway, most of them English dealers, business folk and sharpers and all manner of sly people who thought they could make a few pounds out of the damage done by the Lowland floods. It was not a good omen. There would be coaches and riders along the roads, and crowded bridges, and people demanding to pass through the herd, all of which would cause congestion and consternation. Thurston's collie, which was good at recognising oncoming traffic and creating a channel by parting the animals, would be particularly busy.

Hudson spent most of his time riding between the herd and the castle and the town, and back to the herd, all the time talking to his drivers and to the smith from Bowes, who had proved himself a singular fellow and a great humourist. Everyone's mood was lifted, and even Kerridge permitted himself a thin smile and for once allowed himself some company and a brief visit to the Ancient Unicorn for a meal when Thurston and his collie went off in search of ale and cheese, a fireside, and a jovial landlord. The collie was fed royally outside in the inn's dog pit, while Thurston enjoyed his pipe and Kerridge warmed his feet and dried his clothes inside. Then when Thurston called, the collie joined them, several of the other drovers moving aside to make room for the dog. Soon it slept at their feet, luxuriating in the warmth of the fireside.

At one point Hudson found himself riding back from the old castle to the herd with Swann.

"Kerridge wants to go to America," he said.

"Many do," retorted Swann. "There is little enough work here. The living is poor and the harvest has been poor once again. Many are destitute and the children are hungry. Young Kerridge might be better there."

Hudson could not disagree.

"And then there are the harvest machines, which will put more out of work. Has there been more wrecking in Norfolk?"

"Aye, since you left," said Swann. "Stack burning and wrecking. Hunstanton and Paston way, so they say. The hangman and the transports will be busy."

They rode in silence for a time, admiring the herd from afar, and then Hudson said:

"Sometimes I wonder what is to become of us."

Swann signed noisily, even resignedly.

"You would wonder even more if you saw the machine at Darlington which pulls people in waggons. The steam engine," he said.

"I should like to see it," Hudson said with sudden enthusiasm. "Have you seen it?"

"Aye. One thundering machine with two men pulls twenty waggons and crowds of people at a speed faster than you can ride. It is a vision of Old Nick himself. But go and see it for yourself."

"I cannot imagine what it would be like to travel faster than a horse."

"And I cannot imagine," he said distractedly, "what it would be like for us if they empty the people out of the waggons and fill them full of runts. There would be no more droving, and that is the truth. The machine would do for us and our trade."

Hudson looked at him sharply, for not having seen the machine it was a concept he had not considered. The pair rode in silence for a time, each locked in their own thoughts.

"I am getting old, and everything is changing," Hudson said at last. "I sometimes think they who are blessed are those who can adapt to change. The rest of us struggle with it, and sometimes struggle against it."

As they approached the herd, where Andrew and the others were still busy with the shoeing, and the smoke of the fires mingled with the lowing of the animals, they could hear the high, clear sound of Venning singing as he worked, his voice echoing across the valley:

"I am an old drover, I earn my pay
By tramping this country all over;

With nowhere to stop at the end of the day,
For that is the life of the drover.
When the weather is raining, the journey is long
And the cattle get foot-sore and lazy,
Then I help them along with an old droving song
And I hustle them careful and easy."

Swann said kindly, "Some things never seem to change," and the two grinned at each other and then joined the rest.

In fact the shoeing went on into a third day, but in mid-morning Andrew reported that the smith and his lads had completed the task, and done it well. Hudson paid them off and gave them extra for ale, and slowly the activity died away, the clanging of hammers halted, the fires dulled and spluttered, and the herd lapsed into a mood of drowsy contentment. The kyloes, Andrew said, were in excellent shape and most of the rest, at best a moderate lot, were as good as he thought they would ever be.

Hudson spent the night taking his turn on watch, the dark, damp, impenetrable air chilling his face and hands and with nightmare visions of steam machines filling his mind. But it was also a deeply thrilling vision, and long before the dawn he had decided to leave the herd for a few days and ride the cob to Darlington to see for himself this thing which Swann said might put an end to droving. It was something he could not imagine. But the idea of this new wonder drew him, attracted him, and he knew he might not have a better chance. So after he had slept some more in a hard, cold corner of the castle wall, and then stirred and eaten, he called Andrew, Thurston and Swann to him and outlined his plan. Swann was to set off immediately to hire the forward grazing stances, and tomorrow Andrew and Thurston would get the herd back on to the road. He, intending to visit Darlington, would return in two or three days and rejoin them somewhere near Catterick. They nodded in agreement, though Andrew evidently did not understand Hudson's desire to see the steam machine.

"I'll no risk my life on hot water travelling," he said firmly.

Hudson smiled, but there was one more matter he wanted to discuss. Crawley.

"I am still at a loss to understand Mr Crawley's posturing, and the reasons behind what is happening."

"Tell us what you know," said Thurston, "for I have not met the man."

"He hired me, on Mr Porter's behalf, to bring a drove to Fay's Fair, and Mr Porter, who seems to me an honourable gentleman, arranged the capital and invested it in me on his behalf. I was to buy the herd at Dumfries, but when I arrived in Scotland I found Crawley had rented a large house for a month, that he had invested more of Mr Porter's money in purchasing runts of his own selection, engaged a topsman and several men, and a smith, all without my prior knowledge but in the complete expectation that I was responsible for bringing the drove to Norfolk. It seems to me Mr Crawley's cattle were a very poor choice, and the shoeing was done badly."

"Deliberately badly," Andrew interjected.

"And," Hudson continued, "I suspect that a letter I wrote to Mr Porter may have been intercepted, for I have not received a reply."

Swann, sitting on one of the castle steps, ran his hands through his beard. Then he said he had heard in some bush house or other whispered queries as to Mr Crawley's veracity, but he knew nothing more than that others had marked Crawley as a man to be watched, and not trusted.

"If he deliberately purchased poor stock - and some of the stirks are poor - and then had them poorly shod, is he hoping the herd will not reach St Fay's?" Hudson went on. "And if so, why? Some say it is about land, but I know no more. And I am already looking at some heavy losses."

"I do not know why," Andrew offered. "All I can add is that Mr Crawley searched me out as topsman and then arranged for my creditors to be waiting for me along the way, believing I would not be able to pay them off. I presume he wanted me to suddenly leave the herd and run. You would have had to find another topsman in England."

It was plain no one knew Mr Crawley's motives, and probably never would. But it was also plain Hudson could ill afford further losses and that he desperately needed good prices in Norfolk. Thurston and Andrew promised to keep a close watch on the herd. There seemed little more to be done.

As it was, Andrew had the herd on the move before dawn, the incessant lowing and animal protestations, and the exclamations of the drivers and the excited barking of Thurston's collie, waking Hudson from his reverie and probably waking Bowes, too. Hudson gathered his things and fetched the cob, and when he was quite ready and everything was done, he rode to the crest of the valley just beyond the old castle and saw below him the herd moving sweetly, in threes and fours, a long, thin, dark stream in the mist winding out of the valley and over the hills towards the lower ground to Scotch Corner and beyond. In his head he carried the latest tally (thirteen days gone, 18 animals dropped, the herd now 591), and remembered to write it into his journal before he turned the cob away from the herd and towards Bowes, Barnard Castle, and the hot water machine.

The road provided a very pleasant ride indeed, and the landscape and the morning, which was bright without being warm and gave no sign of the mists which had clouded the hillsides continuously these last few days,

soon put him in a good frame of mind. The weather and the silence, and
the lack of the continual noise of the lowing herd, the shouts of the drivers,
and the barking of Thurston's dog, at first seemed so strange that it was
only with great difficulty that he continually refrained from turning in the
saddle to look behind him to make sure the herd was following. It was so
quiet he could hear birdsong. Gradually, however, the strangeness faded,
and he was left to his own sensibilities and the sound of the cob's hooves
on the good, hard surface of the road. Only one thought clouded his mood.
He was only too aware of the precariousness of his position, in terms of
the debt he would encounter if anything further of an adverse nature occurred to the herd, or if the price fell, and of the fact that, for better or
worse, he had placed a great deal of trust in the Scot. And yet he felt he
could trust Andrew, though he was now very suspicious of Mr Crawley
and his motives and his innumerable hangers-on.

He entered Barnard Castle over the high bridge and saw the good, stone
houses and shops and the spacious market place and thought it a very
bonny place indeed. "I liked it very much, and would have tarried but for
time," he wrote later in his journal. Instead, he walked slowly with the cob
through the market place, enjoying the sunshine and the scene. The market was crowded with townsfolk and a fair sprinkling of traders and
passers-by, travellers like himself. A pair of heavily loaded diligences, each
pulled by teams of six, rolled slowly through the town pursued by three
mangy, excited dogs, and chaises and carts competed for space among the
throng.

In the end he paused at a Piecebridge inn, not far from the green, to rest
the cob and take refreshment, where a drunken stonemason, with his
gnarled, pitted hands and dusty apron, insisted the Romans had named
the place Morbium and had left some ruins hereabouts, though he was
less certain why they should have paused at such a place. So he rode on.
Then, with the sun beginning to descend, Darlington appeared in view,
and with it a change in mood. Now he began to see the smoke of innumerable chimneys and the grime of the factories and mines and smelteries,
and heard, like the sound of approaching doom, the distant rumble of
machinery and the grind of strings of horse-drawn chaldrons as they
groaned and creaked through the yards. The people, too, seemed different, quiet and ragged, cowed and sullen, and he began to wonder if this
was the price extracted by machinery.

Hudson stayed that night at a modest, untidy inn, where at least he had
his own room, a whole bed, and clean linen. Downstairs in the lounge
dirty glasses and plates littered the large central table, the fire had burned
through almost to ashes and the copper pots and saucepans hanging in
serried ranks along the beams were coated with dust. The landlord was

almost as untidy, and just as dirty, and seemed to spend most of his time snoring in a copious armchair or regaling his customers with dubious tales. It seemed most of the work was being done by a couple of lean, busybody maids, local girls by the look of them, and by the landlady, a hard working put-upon sort of woman who scurried continually between the kitchens and the ale rooms, scoulding the maids and shouting instructions to the cook, all the time stepping over the legs of her husband sprawled in his chair.

That evening, over fowl and sausage, tobacco, and ale in a battered pewter tankard, and before retiring, Hudson learned more of the landlord, a man he had come to despise for his laziness, for in the crowded, smoke-filled parlour two Yorkshire drovers, breaking their journey before heading for Slapstones and Sedgeford along the Hambleton road, bowed their heads and lowered their voices to a whisper and told him that ten years before that very same landlord had been most sorely abused. Evidently he had been one of many attending a parliamentary reform meeting in St Peter's Field, Manchester, seemingly a quite peaceful affair, when on the orders of the magistrates the throng was violently attacked by the Manchester Yeomanry, the 15th Hussars and the Cheshire Volunteers, mounted and with sabres drawn. In the confusion and panic as the crowd broke and ran, the landlord received the full force of a swinging blow from the back of sabre full on his skull, and had fallen, and that when he came too he witnessed the hideous scene of eleven people dead and hundreds wounded. Ever since then he had spent his life half lucid, dribbling, idling in his chair while his wife toiled to look after him and the business. It was a tale of great sorrow. Hudson was moved, and said so. Then he asked of the steam machine, and although they had heard it had caused the price of coal to drop from eighteen shillings to twelve shillings, and then eight shillings and sixpence a ton, neither had any useful information. It was only when he spoke to a maid to arrange an early call that he learned where was the best place to go to see the miracle, and at what time. Despite the apprehension, he slept well.

Next day Thomas Hudson stood on the roadway beside the river Skerne in sight of Mr Bonomi's new bridge which gleamed large and clean and bright in the morning air. There were other people there, too, a pedlar and his wife, and some people of fashion in a barouche, a waggon and two carters pulled over to the side with the team grazing lazily on nearby vegetation, a knot of chattering traders, the men in long coats, breeches and porkpie hats, a group of excited, uncontrolled children, a scholarly gentlemen in black leaning on a stick whiling away the time by referring continually to a book, and a group of local wives, their long dresses sweeping the dirt, with their backs to the barouche as though it did not exist. There were more spectators, too, on the far bank of the river, and one or two more of an adventurous type, he could see, who had made their way across the damp meadow beside the river and were now standing beside one of the two smaller arches which flanked the large main arch of the bridge.

How long he stood he did not know - almost an hour, perhaps - but there duly came a time when the horses began to shuffle and twitch, when a ripple of excitement passed through the congregation, and when a faint mechanical sound became discernible, growing ever closer and ever louder. Then there were gasps from the bystanders, and finally he saw it, the cy-lindrical machine with a chimney belching steam and sparks, making an abominable noise the like of which he had not heard before, and behind it a long string of other waggons, some containing people, moving effortless across the bridge and at a speed his cob, or his Jenny, would not have been able to emulate. Hudson gasped with wonder and watched open mouthed as clouds of steam enveloped the bridge and was sucked through the arches down towards the water, and as the machine and its waggons hurtled high over the river. Now he could see the people in the waggons waving, and hear their shrieks. Of terror? He wondered.

Then he was slowly aware of two other things, of some of the traders shaking their fists and waving their sticks at the wonder.

"Damn that Stephenson. Damn his hide. This'll destroy commerce and destroy agriculture. We shall all be peasants and paupers, slaves of ma-chinery," they shouted, amid a ripple of excitement; and aware of the som-bre gentleman in black who had wandered to his side and who was asking, "Was that the Royal George or the Loco Motion?"

Hudson was nonplussed, and could think of nothing to say, and shrugged his shoulders instead. The man wandered away again, book under his arm, and Hudson suddenly remembered Swann's comment that if they took the people out of the waggons and filled them full of runts then the drovers would be out of business, too. He suddenly wanted to say some-thing to the sombre man, but he had gone, and when he looked towards the bridge again the machine had gone also, leaving nothing but a cloud and a sense of awe and excitement trailing in its wake. Now the knots of people were wandering away, talking and arguing among themselves, and all that remained of the spectacle was a few wisps of steam hanging above the Skerne. Once again a silence had descended, the horses settled, and it was all as though nothing had happened and that his eyes had deceived him.

He spent an unsettled and unsettling night.

Not until the day following did Hudson and the cob turn their faces away from Darlington and head out through Scorton towards Catterick, looking for the herd, his mind full of the Loco Motion and of the pleasant expectation of seeing Betty again at Boroughbridge. On the approach to the river Ure the landscape was relatively flat and easy going, he noted, and there was the prospect of plenty of water and grazing, and after he had ridden slowly and easily for most of the day he finally caught up with Venning and the tail of the herd in Leeming Lane, just beyond Roxby House where the old road was wide verged and rutted, and where Swann had arranged the night's grazing. Andrew came to see him straightaway. They had lost one runt, he said, due to exhaustion and gut trouble, and had sold the carcase. But more to the point, they had also lost Faichney.

Hudson felt great sadness, but he was not entirely surprised.

"We went around Catterick to avoid the tollbar," Andrew explained, "but Faichney dropped off without anyone seeing and went on his own into town. When we realised he was missing Macculloch went to search for him and soon found he had been in the Bay Horse Inn. The landlord said that after dark, without knowing what he was doing because of the drink, Faichney had staggered out of the inn, blundered across the green straight into the stream, and had fallen insensible and drowned before anyone found him. It was night-time, of course, and none knew he was missing. In the morning they dragged him out and sent word to the magistrate."

"And what happened?" Hudson asked.

"There was trouble afterwards," Andrew said. "I asked the parson at the church on the hill to bury him, but he said he would not dignify the remains of a drunken wandering Scot who might have died of the plague. I could not talk to him, so I sent Thurston. Thurston paid him some herd money to write the death into the church book, and then paid him for diggers and a funeral. The parson promised he would do it properly and that Faichney would rest near the front wall. I don't know if we can trust him."

The meal that evening was a sombre affair, and that night Hudson slept out in the open, under the stars and within earshot of the soft rustlings and night murmerings of the sleepy herd, and was glad to do so. He was sad about Faichney, and he knew Macculloch was touched, but there was nothing left for them to do. Faichney had fashioned his own fate. So Hudson slept, as lightly as ever, with his ears attuned to the sounds of the dark, dreaming of machines wreathed in cloud.

The herd stirred and began moving at dawn, leaving Faichney to his silent, solitary fate, and made its noisy, mucky, stinking, inquisitive way through the largely empty streets of Boroughbridge before most of the inhabitants were up and about their business. Here there was not much consternation, for Boroughbridge was used to the herds passing through, and used to the ways of the drovers. Once the Great North Road was di-

verted from the old Roman road, bringing the trade and the herds, it became a noted rendezvous for returning Scottish drovers heading north
and a well-known resting place for drovers' collies making their solitary
way from Norfolk back to the glens. Another herd was another herd. Another collie with a scribbled and badly written note on its collar - "Pleze
straw and feed meat will pay latter" - was just another collie. They were
all good for business.

Hudson's mind was only half on the droving, but he saw the long line of
jostling cattle safely through Boroughbridge and on the road to Wetherby
before he wheeled the cob about and rode back into town. The stinking
streets were mottled with slicks of tad, and horses and carts were waiting
patiently at every stopping place, and only now were people beginning to
open their doors and stretch and yawn and make their way outside to
sniff the tainted air and glance at the weather. When he dismounted outside the Black Bull a dull feeling of emptiness, or premonition, overcame
him for the inn looked silent and bolted, with doors and windows still
closed. He wondered if the girl was still safe in the bed they had shared
twice, when he was lonely and she needed to be wanted, and he remembered her sparse room and meagre possessions and the sounds of the day
rattling and chattering outside their window. He also remembered his
overwhelming feeling of guilt and how her face had altered when he told
her he was married, though in truth she had known that from the outset.
Now he knew for certain she was not upstairs in her bedroom.

Then he heard a faint noise at the rear of the building, and duly found a
slatternly girl half-heartedly washing down the cobbled yard. Splashes of
water from the buckets, and from her broom, had soaked the hem of her
tired dress which trailed through the muddy puddles as she worked. When
she saw Hudson a look of dismay crossed her face, but she stopped what
she was doing and waited for him to speak.

"Is Betty here?"

"Who?"

"Betty. The ale girl. She has been here a long time."

The girl with the broom shrugged her shoulders, and continued to stare
at him.

"Is the landlord here?"

She shrugged her shoulders again, but this time inclined her head towards the inn door, indicating he might be inside. Then as if on cue the
landlord himself opened the side door and came out into the yard, partially dressed, yawning and belching. Hudson could smell the interior atmosphere of stale beer and smoke which had seeped into the very timbers
of the place over the decades, and he did not despise it, for he had spent
many comfortable hours in front of the huge fire in the front lounge, with

its low ceilings and polished furniture and shiny, copper pans hanging around the walls. The landlord looked at him as though he knew him, and there was a vague flicker of recognition.

"I want to speak to Betty," Hudson said.

"Now I remember. You had a meal with her in the kitchen a month back," said the landlord.

"I was on my way to Scotland. Is she here now?"

"No. She's gone."

"Where to?"

"Who knows. She packed her roll and left."

"But why? Did something happen?"

The landlord looked bemused, and lowered his gaze.

"Some time after you left a detachment of Dragoons stopped nearby. They looked fine, really fine, with splendid uniforms. And when they rode off again a few days' later she went with one of them. That's all I know."

"Is she coming back?"

Now it was his turn to shrug his shoulders. He did not give the impression that he cared much.

"How should I know. She left me in the morning and I had to find another girl straightaway. It was such a business, such a business. And look what I ended up with." He indicated the grimy girl with the broom.

"But . . . " Hudson began. "Did she mention me at all?"

"She mentioned nobody. She didn't even speak to me before she left. I did not even know she had gone until the ostler told me. Damn the girl," he said angrily.

For a moment Hudson felt lost and defeated, but he knew there was no point in staying. Betty had gone, presumably for good, and there was nothing more for him at the inn. Slowly and almost reluctantly he collected the cob and rode off south in pursuit of the drove, thinking of her brown face and the fall of her hair, and with a heaviness in his heart which was not dispelled until the herd, with a collective sigh, relaxed, gathered itself together and stopped for the night.

They stanced just outside Hopperton on some meadows, a good distance outside the village, which had been rented by Swann because the New Inn had no grazing. And that night, before being called for his night stint watching the herd, and enveloped in a great wave of remorse, he wrote a short letter to his wife, planning to put it on the mail coach in Wetherby.

"Dearest wife," he wrote. "We are making reasonable progress with a poor herd, and there has been a difficulty with the cues. I no longer entirely trust Mr Crawley, and I have had no communication from Mr Porter, which I do not fully understand. These are difficult days. I lost Jenny at the border and have a new cob, and will need good prices at St Fay's to put me in the clear. I hear tell from others on the road the harvest in Norfolk has been but modest, with low returns. Yet fear not. In the fullness of time we shall be together."

He sealed the letter and tried to conjure in his mind a picture of his wife, but he could not, for he could see only Betty.

The night was calm and overcast, with a smell of rain in the air, so the herd was content and quiet, and Hudson and Venning, instead of riding slowly round the fringes of the animals, bedded down on the edge of the meadow near a small copse, wrapped in their greatcoats, their senses alert to every slight noise.

Hudson lit his pipe and found it comforting, and thanked God they had heard no mention of murrain, the news of which usually spread like wildfire along the drove roads, passing from traveller to traveller, coach to coach, and inn to inn, so that the drovers knew when it was about, where it was, and which herds had got it. It was the prospect of rain which made him think of it. Logic told him rinderpest was spawned in dampness and shadow.

There had been an outbreak two years ago which he had managed to avoid by the simple expedient of diverting a herd to Huntingdon, away from the Fens where it was rampant, but he had always been frightened of it. Rinderpest could wipe out thousands of animals with so little effort, and there was nothing to be done except isolate the runts into groups, dispose of the dead, and pray for healing sunshine. He had listened in silent horror to old drovers who told such awful tales of the murrain, and to the old man in Holt who once, and at Hudson's instigation, recalled that his forebear had been financially wiped out by the 1747 outbreak when the St Faith's and Scotland droves were devastated and when frightened, determined gangs from towns and villages attacked approaching herds on the road to force them to turn away. That year the green lanes and raiks all the way from Norfolk to Galloway were littered with the carcases of dead animals left to rot where they fell. Then he thought about the Loco Motive machine which could wipe out the droving business completely. Later, he forgot all about rinderpest and steam, and it did not rain that night, and Hudson, like the herd, slept lightly.

In fact it did not rain next day either, though there was no doubt the weather had changed. The morning mists now had a distinctly chilly edge, and as soon as they cleared then banks of cloud rolled in, so that there was no warmth anywhere. To add to their woes Macculloch found two more stirks with loose cues, but Venning and Thurston, who had a hammer, spare cues and nails in his pouch, managed to re-nail them without causing too much consternation among the herd. Once they met a bagman with bulging sample satchels, and said "good-day." Then Swann appeared with instructions on a stance south of Wetherby and with the news that Tait's drove was only two days' ahead and that they might have to pass him if they wanted the better grass. It seemed an unlikely prospect. Aware of time passing, and the need for good grazing, Hudson did not want to push the herd hard, for he knew many of them lacked quality and some were already showing signs of losing weight. It was a careful balance he had to maintain.

Slowly and mournfully the drove streamed on, and by noon the animals' heads began to drop as weariness and a need for water overcame them. Only Thurston's collie remained as energetic as it had been that morning. As for the drovers, they were able to refresh themselves momentarily, as the herd poured by, at the Old Fox Inn, a mile from Wetherby, where the sign hanging in a chestnut tree swung gently too and fro in the breeze. Then with the stance practically in sight they suffered a major delay. Thurston led the lead animals of the herd up to the Wetherby bar, only to be confronted by a tiresome dandy pikeman inflated by his not inconsiderable importance. Indeed, he was in a full uniform of canary yellow, a black, glazed hat, corduroy trousers and white stockings.

Thurston shouted to him to open the gate, but the official would have none of it, and did everything slowly and deliberately.

"How many creatures?" he asked standoffishly when he finally strolled across.

"Over five hundred, and five ponies," Thurston replied with mounting impatience as the herd began to push and congregate around him. "And hurry man, we cannot hold them forever."

"How many exactly?"

"I do not have an exact number. Five hundred and sixty, perhaps."

"It is one shilling and sixpence a score, and I shall need to know how many," retorted the pikeman, who by this time had been joined by two assistants.

"I don't know exactly how many. Just open the gate," said Thurston with mounting frustration, for by now the herd was pressing hard and the numbers were swelling on the lane behind him.

"Then they will have to be counted," the pikeman replied with due solemnity. He stood to one side and positioned himself beside the gatepost while his two assistants unlatched the gate, carefully opening it a short distance and then holding it firmly in a half closed position so that only one animal at a time could pass through. An hour later, with the pikeman still counting, only a third of the drove had passed through the gate, and those that had were being held together as best they could by Kerridge and Pearse. But by now the runts were restless and were beginning to break free on either side of the gate and wander afield in search of grass. The drivers and the collie struggled to contain them, but despite Hudson's anguished protestations the pikeman would not change his way. The herd had to be tallied, one at a time. Then there was further alarm when, from the opposite direction, there appeared along the road first a jagger with his talbot and a train of upwards of twenty ponies, followed closely, and with much pomp and cacophony, by two persons of quality in a chariot drawn by four matching horses. One of the two postillians, a negro, jumped down from the rear as the vehicle slowed behind the string of pack animals, and ran to the pikeman and gave him something. The effect was immediate. The herd had to be held and cleared off the road and the gate opened to allow the chariot and the train through before counting could resume. And this is precisely what happened. By now the runts had spilled out on both sides of the road and Hudson's men were in grave danger of losing control, but gradually they were gathered together, the gate was closed save for the small gap, and the tally resumed. Finally, Hudson was able to pay him, but not a word passed between them.

Four hours after they had first reached the bar Venning gratefully nursed the vanguard on to Swann's stance in Scotch Lane outside Wetherby, where there were shoeing shops, dog pits, ample water and reasonable grass. For the tired and irritable drivers there was accommodation of sorts at a row of villainous looking cottages, though only Macculloch and Pearse took up the offer, the remainder preferring to sleep and eat outside, beside the herd.

Hudson saw the drove settled and then walked into town, to place his letter on the mail coach and to see if there had been any word from either Mr Crawley or Mr Porter, though he sensed, correctly as it turned out, that there would not. The town, as ever, was thronged with tradesfolk and coaches and livestock. The old drovers' inn, the Spotted Ox, was full to the beams, as was the Swan & Talbot, while the stables and pens at the rear of The Angel seethed with horses and noise. Smiths and stable lads, preparing for the imminent arrival of the London-Glasgow coach, in the midst of its forty-hour journey, busied themselves with teams and harness and fodder, traders and dealers clamoured and argued, and passing soldiers wandered haphazardly by in pairs and took in the sights. Later, his letter delivered, Hudson strolled to the riverside to look at the bridge, its six arches gleaming with white stone after the recent rebuilding, and he thought what a fine, bustling place Wetherby was, full of traders, well-to-do's and soldiery, and how his pulse was always quickened by its constant activity and growing sense of importance.

When Hudson returned to Scotch Lane, however, and saw Andrew and Thurston and two or three others standing in a little group in the gathering gloom talking quietly among themselves, he knew something was wrong. Thurston waited until he approached, then turned from the others, faced him, and said matter-of-factly, "Kerridge has gone."

"Gone? Gone where?"

"He has left the drove and gone off on foot."

"Where to? Why?"

"To Liverpool. The lad wanted to take ship to America. He was determined. We could not talk him out of it."

"Did he have money?"

Thurston dropped his gaze, and was clearly implicated. "Yes, he has some," he said at last. "He had three pounds saved, and Bell gave him two more pounds for his fare, to help him on his way. I gave him three pounds I had saved to help with his keep."

"He was determined to go," Andrew said. "The wee lad would have gone at one time or other, for he has had his fill of England. Macadam the road man went to America, and came back full of ideas and made his fortune. Perhaps Kerridge will be the same."

"But why did he go now?"

"He was determined."

"No, I mean at this time of year. There are no boats now. He will have to find winter work in Liverpool and wait for passage in the spring," Hudson exclaimed.

"I do not think he understood that," Thurston said. "None of us did. He will have to wait for spring?"

Hudson was certain the sailing season from Yarmouth to Quebec did not commence until April or May, and he presumed it was the same for Liverpool.

"Yes, he will have to wait," he muttered sadly.

There was nothing more to be said. The lad had gone and they could not fetch him back. The men wandered off in different directions, each to his own thoughts. Only later did it occur to Hudson that he was now two drivers short, and although neither Andrew or Thurston had said anything, because they knew money was scarce, it was clear he would have to put the matter right.

He pulled his greatcoat around him and stared into the coldness of the night. It was too late to do anything now, but he could recruit in Retford. Yes. He would recruit in Retford in four days' time.

The next three days were hard, but they passed well despite the fact they had to ride rather than walk, because there were fewer men and because the herd seemed to sense a certain urgency. In resolute mood, therefore, they passed through Bramham and moved on by Milford and Scawsby, where Swann had reserved a useful stance with unusually good grass, which surprised Hudson because he knew Tait was ahead with his herd and that he would also have been scouring the district for quality grazing. A lengthy pack trail on a narrow causey beside the Great North Road threaded beside them heading north, and east of Doncaster they met three drunken drovers and their dogs on the road, also heading north, and heard the news that there had been a hanging in Lincoln which evidently drew huge crowds. Then there was a delay north of Bawtry when the herd became entangled with a heavily laden diligence which was leaning haphazardly to one side, because something was broken, and with a mail coach with a noisy, impatient guard, which was delayed because of the mishap. Somehow they channelled the herd into the small gap between the two vehicles, and passed through, but it all took a long time and they were exhausted by the time Hudson finally called a halt early in the afternoon.

On the road to Torworth, Hudson had another decision forced upon him. He could keep the herd on a direct line south to follow the Old North Road; he could take them along the Great North Road, which now diverted into Retford and passed right through the town; or he could turn east through Hayton and along the old green lanes and tracks. It made sense to follow the latter course because it would avoid the town and all the difficulties inherent in moving a large herd, and it would put them on the shorter line for Newark. And it was on these facts that he based his decision. In consequence he instructed Venning, who happened to be in the lead, to turn them east at Torworth on to the old road to Lound over the marshes, and then over the Chesterfield Canal at Townend Bridge. Shortly afterwards, however, everything fell apart.

The attack, when it came, was as sudden and fierce as it was unexpected. With the canal behind, and at the point where the landscape turned hilly and where they had begun to climb the slopes of Hollinhill, Venning turned the herd south once again on to some of the tracks that hugged the little valleys and headed towards Clarborough. The endless slopes tired the herd, and slowed them to little more than an amble, and as they approached Clarborough Hill, with the herd now strung out over an even greater distance, Hudson began to experience a prickle of concern that they would not be able to keep an eye on them all.

Approaching the slopes, where there was open land on one side and copses and patches of woodland on the other, Venning could see smoke up ahead, and a tumbled, ruinous wall beside the track behind which three labourers seemed to be stoking a number of fires with waste evidently cut from lower down the slopes. If the herd smelled the smoke it did not register the fact, because the cattle could not actually see the flames, and the breeze, what there was of it, was carrying the clouds away from them. So Venning took the front of the herd along by the wall, and glanced over and nodded at the men, who seemed unusually preoccupied, though he thought nothing of it, and the runts tramped on. And so the herd passed by the wall, or most of it, for quite suddenly, and with about a hundred head, with Pearse at the rear, still to go, three, four or perhaps five bundles of blazing material, one after the other, came hurtling over the wall right into the centre of the line of animals. The bundles hit the ground with considerable force and burst apart, sending blazing clumps flying in all directions, as though the track itself was on fire, obliterating the view with clouds of choking smoke.

The herd was terrified. There was a brief suspended moment of inaction, when the animals closest to the flames were halted in their tracks. Then a look of fear leapt into their eyes.

As it turned out it was more of a scattering than a stampede. The runts closest to the flames screamed in terror and turned the only way they could, on to the open land away from the wall, and then the lowing and the fright swept through the entire herd. The panic was total, and acting almost as a single entity the entire herd pushed and pressed and scrambled in all directions away from the flames and away from the road and the wall. Hudson and the others, taken by surprise at the sudden onset of chaos, took matters in at a glance, then wheeled their mounts and raced to catch the leaders of the rush, to turn them back. But there followed long moments of panicking runts, pushing and jostling, of smoke and flames, of brief glimpses of other riders and horses, and of noise.

Long minutes later - perhaps twenty minutes later - Hudson's men finally regained control, channelling the herd across the pasture beside the wall and then, when they were well clear of the blazing bundles, which were still burning, back on to the track. Three hours later, the excitement and the panic having subsided, the herd was finally contained, quiet and restful, on the slopes of Cowsland Hill. The men met together at last, exhausted by their efforts, aware there had been other riders among the herd, taking advantage of the panic and the smoke.

"We have lost some," Hudson said grimly to Andrew. "We'd best do a tally immediately."

They did what they could, moving among the animals slowly and quietly, dividing them into groups so that they could count, and yet doing it without reintroducing the uncertainty of the afternoon which, if it took hold, could spread yet again like the flames from the fires. Even so, darkness was falling by the time they had finished and by the time five of them had taken their positions to keep watch through the night. Hudson gathered together the tally sticks in the gathering gloom and sorted through them. If the count was accurate, then two of the runts were injured, presumably in the rush and panic, and about sixteen were missing. There was no point in looking for them in the dark. The attack had been well organised, and the runts would have been led away by horsemen who knew the local countryside and who would have a slaughterer waiting somewhere ready to do his work by lantern light.

"We must stay here and do another tally in the morning, to make sure," Hudson said to Thurston shortly before they settled down for the night on the damp grass beside a hedgerow, "and then I will report it in Retford, and recruit some more men."

Thurston, his collie curled beside him, mumbled in the dark.

"This is a hanging affair," Hudson said, who was also aware that if the tally was right he would be fortunate to even recover his costs at St Fay's. In any event, he went to sleep recalling that he was several days' behind with his journal, and with Crawley very much in his mind.

Hudson awoke thirsty and chilled to the bone, when the rills and clefts of Cowsland Hill were still obscured by mist and the dusky remnants of night. As soon as he stirred, and as soon as there was sufficient light, he knew the tally was all important, and after taking a tot of warming whisky and a handful of oatmeal soaked in cold water, he kicked the others awake and set them about the business of counting. The night crew reported no activity, and because of a low cast sky and an obscured moon, very little movement in the herd, either, and soon they were all busy with the tally sticks. It was a long, laborious, humdrum business, and in the end it confirmed the worst fears of the previous day. Sixteen runts were missing. The only marginally good news was that the two injured animals seemed to have recovered, or at any rate, would recover. One or two others bore slight marks of singeing from the flames, but the memory of that would soon fade even if their inbred fear of fire would not. In any event it made sense to stay where they were for the day, to settle the herd further, and to report the matter to the authorities. He wondered whose land they were on, but saw no distinguishing marks or signs, and hoped that Swann, when he heard of the misadventure, would come back and settle matters with the landowner. The rest would lose them another day's travelling, and lose him more money in expenses, but there was little alternative. He needed to inform the authorities of the crime, he needed extra men, and he could not arrange either with the herd on the move for the simple reason he was short of drivers. So he gathered the men together, discussed the situation, told them to stay with the herd, and keep vigilant, and shortly before noon set off for Retford with Thurston at his side.

All the way along the track from Cowsland to Retford, which recent rains had turned into a narrow corridor of cloying mud, Hudson unconciously searched the grass verges for any sign of the movement of riders and cattle, but there were none save for an occasional footprint or the grooves of cart wheels. He presumed the raiders had anticipated a hurried communication with Retford and had sensibly headed off in some other direction; but nonetheless, he was disappointed. They passed three or four country people trudging the messy road, heading towards Retford, but all of them shook their heads and turned away at Hudson's questioning. At another point they met a solitary rider, wearing leather jackboots up to his hips and a thick riding cloak, but the man, far from offering advice or information, seemed more concerned that he might be in the middle of a hold-up of his own and that his saddlebags might be in danger. He, too, had no information to offer, having seen nothing and spoken to no-one. Recognising the futility of further questioning, Hudson and Thurston rode on in silence, having bid the man nervous farewell, and they finally parted in the Market Place, Hudson bound for the town hall and Thurston to search the inns for likely new recruits. But even Thurston, who had told his collie to stay with the herd, had kept his own counsel, concerned that the drove was on the brink of financial disaster, worrying how Hudson was planning to pay his way.

Retford, a noisy and bumptious place at the best of times, seemed to have grown in importance every time he had seen it, and Hudson recognised its bustling confidence and burgeoning commercial status now that traffic from the Great North Road constantly poured through the centre. There were travellers and tourists, busy tradespeople and business people, ruffians and sharpers, and a constant stream of coaches and carts, and yet it seemed to him this was simply the crust on a very mixed pie. Beneath the crust, small groups of the ragged poor stood around, uncertain what to do or where to go, the shadows of poverty, hopelessness and the workhouse stretching towards them, silently watching the ever changing street scene. And away from the market place there were rows and clusters of the most foul hovels which would have to be cleared away sooner or later.

Hudson left the cob at the White Hart and pushed his way through the pavement hubbub as a coach from Edinburgh, bound for London, paused to unload passengers while another, a Royal Mail coach, waited for its team to be changed and the hotel's Boots to finish loading the luggage. Passers-by and ostlers and horses, important passengers, stable lads, boys and dogs and coachmen all milled around the entrance, talking, fidgeting, shouting and complaining and generally doing their best to ignore the piles of luggage congregated on the footpad. It took Hudson only a few

moments to ascertain from a harrassed hotel barman that the town's officials had already partaken of their midday sustenance and had returned
to their offices.

The town hall was opposite the White Hart, and connected to it by a low
covered bridge through which waiters and barmen could cross to and fro,
responding to orders from the aldermen and the clerks, without ever allowing food to go cold in the rain or dust to waylay the drinks. Hudson
went into the hall through the main ground floor door, but even here there
were people milling around in the corridors, talking at once, and congre-
gating outside the doors to the various rooms. There seemed to be a sort of
tension in the air, and several times he heard the word "cholera." Finally,
he inquired of a louche, thin-faced gentleman leaning disinterestedly
against the wall, idly slapping a bamboo wand against one of his immacu-
lately polished boots, "What is happening here?"

"The peasantry are panicking. They think cholera will soon strike them
dead," he said, casting a distainful glance over the melee in the passageway.

"Is there cholera in the town?"

"No, not that I am aware of. But they all expect it at any time. Some say
it breeds in the poor houses, which need firing, others that it travels along
the Great North Road. I say neither. I say they need a cholera hospital. But
the aldermen are fools and brigands. They do not listen to advice."

The man ran his eyes over Hudson, noted his damp clothes and his mud
clogged boots, and smelled the smell of animals, and recognised him immediately for what he was.

"You have beasts to sell at the town hall?" he asked, with an amused
smile on his face.

"No, I have come to report a crime. Who should I see?"

"Oh," said the man off-handedly, "the officials are so full of cholera fever they will have no interest in crimes. The last real crimes we had here
were those of bribery, during the elections, and all they could think of then
was to call out the troops."

"But is there no-one?"

"I suggest you try Alderman Meekley, but I doubt if you will be allowed
to penetrate his rooms any further than his clerical man."

The stranger, as it turned out, was right. Hudson pushed his way through
the animated, chattering throng, located Mr Meekley's offices, wormed
his way through, and was halted at the first hurdle by a miserable clerk
sitting at a desk littered with letters and documents, seals and pens and
ink pots and all the paraphenalia of administration. Hudson explained his
problem, and told him of the raid on the herd. To give him his due, the
clerk at least listened intently.

"I will pass on the information to the Alderman," he said abruptly before returning to his letters.

"But can you do nothing?"

"Nothing, for the moment. Soon, it will be the wish of the Alderman to appoint watchmen and two constables, to be paid out of Corporation Funds no less, but it is not yet appropriate to do so as guidance regulations for such constables have not yet been drawn up," he said by way of explanation. "And if you ask me, they will not be drawn up for some time. Matters such as these need great deliberation. Now, if you will excuse me."

The clerk returned to his documents, and other people with equally urgent communications pushed past Hudson to present their claims. For a time the exhausted drover stood and absorbed the scene. Sometimes an important person was admitted to Alderman Meekley's room, and sometimes, above the hum and babble, he could hear voices murmuring behind the closed door. But after a quarter of an hour, and being no closer to an audience with his quarry, Hudson finally decided to cut his losses. He pushed his way through the throng once again, attracted the clerk's attention by tapping him on a shoulder, looked him straight in the eyes and said, "You will tell him? About the assault on my herd?"

For a moment the clerk looked perplexed.

"The assault on my herd and the theft of my cattle."

Then he recalled the matter.

"Oh, yes. Yes, yes. I will tell him. But at the moment it is impossible. It is the cholera question," said the clerk, throwing his arms in the air in the French manner, in a gesture of hopelessness.

Irritated beyond words, Hudson nevertheless recognised the futility of his mission, so he collected the cob from the White Hart, crossed the Idle river and walked into Bridgegate, through the crowd in the cheese market, and entered Ye Olde Sun, where he knew he would find Thurston. Hudson liked the place, with its lath and plaster walls, steep roof and curiously narrow upper storey, and he liked the people who generally frequented it. They were of a kind, drovers, poor tenant farmers, wheelwrights, masons. All of them craftsmen, skilled at their profession, none of them rich. He felt comfortable in their company, felt one of them, and he saw them as equals.

Sure enough, he found Thurston sitting on his own in quiet contemplation a corner of the crowded parlour, taking his time with his ale. Hudson summoned the serving girl, purchased a mug of ale and replenished Thurston's mug. Then he told him of the events at the town hall and of the hopelessness of persuading anyone to do anything about it.

Thurston nodded, as though he had suspected it.

"We must look after ourselves," he said.

"That we must," Hudson replied.

"Pistols? Shall we purchase pistols?"

Hudson thought for a moment, and then rejected the idea. He shook his head.

"No, but we will get extra drivers. Have you had any success?"

"Yes, I have engaged two men, one of whom I know as a reliable fellow, and the other recommended by him. They have already gone on to the herd, and you will meet them when we return."

"That is good news. It will be a great help."

"But even they will not help us if the reivers attack again. The Scot, Bell, is a big man, but even he was battered yesterday when he tried to intervene," Thurston warned.

"Then we must move the herd out of the area as quickly as possible," Hudson said. "Before first light."

Later that night, and before cloud finally obscured the moon, Hudson drew out his journal and concentrated hard on bringing matters up to date, inscribing at the end of the passage the miserable tally: twenty-three days gone, thirty-five head lost, herd now 574. He closed the journal, wrapped it carefully, and put it away securely in his bag. Gloomily, he knew the figures represented a prescription for financial disaster.

In the darkness of the night, listening to the shuffling and small noises of the herd, Hudson determined to reach Bourne and the theoretical safety of the Fens in three days, which would mean pushing the herd hard. It was a chance he had to take, for the irate owner of the land on which they had taken up their unauthorised stance had, only the day before, exacted a substantial payment from Andrew "for the inconvenience," and was clearly set on doing so again if they lingered in the locality. And in the darkness Thurston brought the two new men to meet him, Matthew Kiddiman, from Cromer, the son of a fisherman, who had turned his back on the sea, and Taylor Livock, who had run away from his Suffolk home some years ago and had not returned. Hudson knew neither of them, but Thurston said Kiddiman was honest and that Livock seemed likewise, so they settled the matter of wages and shook hands on it. Both were on foot, but they had worked herds before and knew what was expected of them, and it was not long before they were absorbed into the routine.

The rest of the night was cold and chill, and all their clothes were wet with dew, but they stirred early, before it was properly light, and eased the herd into the first sluggish movement of the day just as the first streaks of light were beginning to appear on the dawn sky. All day, and with barely a break, the herd trudged through Headon and Markham, the men all the time watching the surrounding fields and woods, expecting an attack but seeing nothing, and in the end Hudson kept them going until early evening and until they had waded the shallow river Trent, where they found pasture and a place where the men could sink down in exhaustion and the herd could water and graze.

Kiddiman and Livock had acquitted themselves well, and proved useful, and Hudson was pleased, even more so when Swann suddenly appeared, his beard matted with mud and moisture after a hard ride, to see the scheme of things.

"I am going to Bourne," Hudson said. "I feel safer out of this area, and in the Fens."

Swann agreed. He could arrange stances at Old Somerby, beyond Grantham, and at Bourne, but it was a hard two days' walk.

"We will be there," Hudson said. "Arrange it." Then he asked after Tait and his drove, but Swann had not seem him.

"He has gone through Bennington towards Grantham, because a landlord told me, but that was two days' ago. He may be at Stamford by now."

That night they mounted extra watches on the edges of the herd and hoped the overcast and threatening skies would keep the animals together. And so it proved. There was no movement all night, and no attack, and they saw no-one abroad in the darkness except one traveller with an exhausted mount which splashed along the edges of the river heading for Newark. The man nodded at Venning, who happened to be closest and, not wishing to disturb the runts, said no more and carried on without stopping.

Over the evening meal Bell and Kiddiman, who were meant to be sleeping, began a conversation when Bell began to sing quietly "Ye Banks and Braes." When he stopped, Kiddiman said he had heard stories of Rob Roy MacGregor, and was it true he once went to Norfolk?

"Aye, they do say so, in 1705 or thereabouts, and I dare say there were some runts at the bottom of it. He was a rogue, but they do say he was a gentle one, for they gave him a bonny funeral. But he no thought twice about reiving. It was how they lived then," Bell explained.

"How was that?"

"There were no roads in the Trossachs in those days, and no English spoken, so cattle were at the heart of everything. You had to pay blackmail to take a herd through clan territory, and there was a lot of reiving and raiding and fighting. They were all rogues in those days."

"But did he come to Norfolk?" asked the inquisitive Kiddiman, intrigued at the thought.

"Aye, maybe he did, perhaps to St Faith's. There are so many stories about him."

Bell passed over his whisky, allowing Kiddiman to take a draught, and with that they settled down to sleep, Kiddiman with coloured visions of Rob Roy in his mind.

When they woke in the quiet hour shortly before dawn and stirred in their rolls and greatcoats it was to find the weather had changed yet again. This time there was the clear, distinct smell of rain in the air. The wind had picked up a little, too, and by the time the herd began to move, and Newark was behind them, it had begun to fall, gently at first and then, as daylight increased, with increasing force and regularity.

The landscape was flatter now, and more like the Fens, but Hudson urged them unmercifully towards Grantham, the wet, black line snaking and twisting in tune to the banks of the swollen river Witham; and then towards Somerby, where they stanced for the night; but it was a head-down day of miserable, unrelenting rain, lanes and tracks churned to ankle deep mud, soaked greatcoats, and the stink and noise of a tired herd on the road. The stance was just as bad, some wet meadows just beyond the road, where those who were not on watch all night were hard pressed to find shelter. Eventually, most of them bedded down in the lee of a hedgerow, covering themselves completely with their greatcoats, trying to shut out the noise of the shuffling herd and the relentless pounding of the rain.

Gradually, towards dawn, it began to ease, and once again Hudson had them on the road early, and before any of the drivers had eaten, so that they were forced to try to have a mouthful of oatmeal as they moved.

By midday they had crossed the East Glen river and were streaming towards Hawthorpe, the inhabitants of that tiny community standing by the doors of their homes as the herd pushed and shuffled and bellowed its way through, and then, shortly after Bell spotted in the distance the gleaming stone walls of Grimsthorpe Castle, and called out to the others to look at it, and at the old Black Horse Inn on the main road, they slithered gratefully down the last of a series of tiring little hills and between woody copses inhabited by clouds of nervous pheasants, and saw Bourne spread before them, dull and grey in the watery light.

Hudson got the exhausted herd safe and stanced before he turned the cob towards town, calling at several of the inns and bush houses to see if there were any messages, but it was to no avail. There was nothing, no word from Porter or Crawley, nothing but a short note from Swann to say he had gone on to Whaplode Drove to arrange grazing and a stance before they reached Wisbech, and would wait there for further instructions. Hudson was reassured. At least Swann had encountered no further difficulties, and as there had been no further attempt to interfere with the herd he began to wonder if they had now left the danger of another attack behind them. On the other hand, the depleted herd was now utterly exhausted after three hard days of tramping through mud and rain. And there were not enough of them of sufficient average weight to pay all the expenses of the drove, unless prices at St Fay's rose above those of last year. And he did not expect that to happen.

His hopes of a respite were dashed, however, as he stood in the market place contemplating his next move, when a complete stranger, a travelling salesman to judge by his muddy apparel, and a man of jovial appearance with a round, bewhiskered face, appeared beside him and introduced himself as John Dewing, a seller of coach and livery lace and other fringe materials, from Dove Street in Norwich. He had with him a leather travelling bag, which he placed on the ground between them. Hudson wondered if it was full of lace and fripperies for the wealthy to decorate their carriages, but refrained from asking.

"I am led to believe, from careful observation and from my considerable knowledge of human nature," he said, "that you are the very man I have been seeking, namely, Mr Thomas Hudson, drover, who is occupied at this very time in bringing a herd from Scotland to Norfolk. Would my surmise be correct?"

"You are correct," Hudson replied, whereupon the stranger's mood darkened. He touched Hudson lightly on the elbow and guided him in a slight sideways direction so that they were facing the wall of a nearby building rather than the street and the passers-by.

"I do not wish to be seen engaging in nefarious activity," said Mr Dewing, in a quiet and serious voice, "but I am bidden to carry a message to you, a message, so I am told, of considerable urgency."

"Who from?"

"Your man Swann. Mr Isaac Swann, a most genial and hearty fellow I may say."

"Where did you see him? I have just received a note from him from Whaplode Drove."

"In Wisbech. I should explain that I am travelling to our more important country towns and am currently on my way to Stamford, to pursue my calling, but I met Mr Swann - whom I knew vaguely, I should add - in Wisbech. He knew I was travelling to Bourne, and he asked me if I would be the carrier of an urgent message should I happen to see you along the way. I have been looking out for a herd, and have seen only one, which was not you, but having observed you in the street here, I was persuaded I had found the right man."

"You have indeed. And the message?"

Mr Dewing, by now thoroughly relishing his role as a conveyor of secrets, looked about him with exaggerated care and suspicion, and then turned his face towards Hudson and lowered his voice to a whisper.

"Mr Swann asked if I would tell you that you will almost certainly face difficulties with the herd at Setchey. He has heard there are men, whom he did not name, who are waiting there and who are certainly up to no good. He said you will know about them, and suggests you find an alternative route. Setchey is a place to be avoided, he said."

"Did he say who these men are?"

"Something to do with a Mr Crawley, apparently. Wanting money and up to no good, I'll be bound."

The thought of another attack on the herd plunged the drover further into despair, and he knew his only chance was to out-think and out-manoeuvre those determined to stop him and his herd reaching Norfolk.

Hudson thanked the man and questioned him further about Swann, and, finally convinced that both Mr Dewing and the message were genuine, offered to buy him dinner, or at least a little wine, just for his trouble, but Mr Dewing would have none of it.

"I have done my duty, sir, " he said, "my public duty. It is the very least I can do." And with that he picked up his bag and wandered nonchalantly across the market place, presumably looking for buyers of coach lace.

Hudson watched him go, and then went to collect the cob to ride back to the herd. He was now twenty-six days into the drove, faced by further difficulties, and already in serious debt.

A difficult night produced largely clear skies, a brisk wind and a bright moon, and maybe a touch of frost in the shadowy hollows of the stance. Enough to chill, anyway. But the herd was too tired to wander very far in the unaccustomed light, so they stayed sullenly where they were. As he and the cob quietly plodded around the perimeter of the drove, it gave Hudson time to think, time to prepare for who or whatever was waiting at Setchey, and when Andrew finally came to see him at first light he had already decided upon a plan of action. The two stood together in the shadow of a small, dark copse, where the wind was less, and whispered quietly together.

"We will carry on, and maintain the idea that the herd is definitely on its way to Setchey," Hudson said. "Venning is sensible and will keep his mouth shut, and he can borrow a pony. Send him ahead to make contact with Swann, to tell Swann to arrange stances at Whaplode Drove and Wisbech and Setchey, as though we are coming through that way. He might also be able to make contact with Tait, to enlist his help, to spread the word in Setchey that we are three or four days' behind."

"And then?"

"Then I want you and Thurston and the rest to turn the herd east to Spalding and along the ridge towards the estuary. You will have to make your own arrangements, as best you can, but there is a good stance at Sutton, at Docking's Halt, and they know me at the Cock and Magpie Inn and at the Bull. You can pick up supplies there. I know the landlords, so make use of my name. Then you will have to send ahead to engage the guide, Wigglesworth, to take the herd over the estuary at the earliest suitable low water. Once across and in Norfolk, push on to Swaffham as quickly as possible."

"And you?"

"I will stay in Bourne for two days, to give you a reasonable start, and then make my way to Setchey, telling everyone the herd is a day behind me. I will see what Crawley's men intend, and somehow delay them, to give you time to get through Lynn. Hold the herd at Swaffham, and I will meet you there as soon as I can."

"I sense an element of risk here," Andrew said quietly.

"On the estuary? Yes, of course, but Wigglesworth will get you across safely. He is a good man, and is related to a drover. He knows the ways of herds."

"No, I meant at Setchey. You do not know who these people are, or what they intend to do. You must not go alone."

"I have to go alone. I cannot see any other way. Venning and Swann will already have gone ahead and I shall be in Bourne. You will need everyone else with the herd. There is no one else to spare to come with me. This is also something I have to face alone. Remember, hold the herd at Swaffham for news of the prices at St Fay's. I will meet you there again as soon as I can be free of these ruffians."

Andrew nodded, giving his tacit approval, and for several minutes they discussed details. An hour later, as the rest of the men and the herd began to stir, and as Hudson collected his things together and prepared the cob, he saw Venning on a borrowed pony slip away from the edge of the herd and head out along the track towards Deeping Fen and the Crowland marshes in search of Swann and Tait, to prepare them to lay a false trail, and he watched from a distance as Andrew and Thurston stood together in quiet conversation, and then as they briefed the other drivers.

As Hudson rode slowly into Bourne and searched for a bed for the night, and arranged his accommodation, Andrew and Thurston urged the exhausted herd on through the bleak, bitter cold dampness of the Fens, with the filled dykes and implicit threat of flooding, by squalid and lonely ague and opium-ridden hovels half hidden beside towering embankments, and into the teeth of a saw-edged wind. Past Pickworth's Drove, and despite the drivers' urgings, the herd moved slower and slower, and it was very late in the day when the long black snake finally straggled across Spalding's bridge over the Welland river and found a stance near Weston. By the time the mass of runts had settled for the night Venning had already caught up with Swann, at Throckenholt, and explained Hudson's instructions, while Hudson himself had settled impatiently into a modest inn on the edge of Bourne. Outside, the wind buffeted the trees and shook down the last of the leaves, so that they scurried and rattled around the roads and lanes, and cut with knife-edge cold into anyone who ventured abroad after dark.

Next morning Hudson stayed sensibly where he was, beside a good blaze at the inn, thinking of his wife alone in Norfolk, and of Crawley, and as he did so it happened that Venning and Swann, as planned, were making their way to Wisbech, which at that time was agog with abolitionist excitement, and then towards St German's, telling everyone as they travelled of the large drove which was but two days' away. Thurston and Andrew, meanwhile, nursed the actual herd through Holbeach, past the Horse and Groom Inn, as far as Docking's Halt and the Cock and Magpie, where they purchased supplies, and then sent a message ahead for Wigglesworth, the guide.

Thurston was acutely aware it was not an ideal time to take a herd across the estuary, because of the current works. Hundreds of labourers, many of them Irish, were busy in the locality digging the new river outfall and constructing the huge causey which would one day carry a new road all the way from Lincolnshire into Norfolk. In consequence, the banks of the estuary seethed with activity, machinery, horses, waggons and men, which meant drunken gangs were wandering the neighbourhood looking for gain and spreading smallpox and cholera, and thieving and violence was rife. In consequence, Sutton was a place which had recoiled in upon itself, guarded, suspicious, protective. The last thing on townsfolks' minds was a large herd of scrawny Scottish runts and drunken drovers coming through. But there was no alternative. The causey was not yet open, and the herd would have to rely on the ageing Wigglesworth to get them across the estuary.

On the second morning, which was again bright and crisp and touched with frost, Hudson packed his bag, paid his bill and bid farewell to mine host and his wife at the inn, and then turned the cob towards Crowland and Wisbech, a town of pretty buildings and windmills. However, it was Setchey which was uppermost in his mind, and he could not help wondering what was awaiting him there. In his mind's eye he pictured the miserable, riotous, churchless village, the brewery beside the river and the three or four victuallers, and smiled at the thought of an earlier description he had heard which ascribed to it "thirteen houses and fourteen cockolds."

In any event it was the place the herds had to go through to get into Norfolk, simply because they had to cross St German's bridge in the dreadful Fens. These thoughts occupied him for much of the morning and did little to lighten the enormous load, mainly financial, he felt was pressing him down. Nevertheless, by the time Hudson reached Crowland, the herd, under the direction of Wigglesworth and his grey horse, was already making its edgy, anxious way through the raucous chaos of the labouring gangs, the milling of waggons, horses and machinery, and over the leg-sapping, oozing mud bottom of the estuary towards Cross Keys on the far Norfolk bank.

"This is the end of guiding, and the end of me" Wigglesworth said to Andrew at one point, eyeing the lenghtening line of the new causeway.

"Aye," retorted Andrew, "and the bottom of my pockets, too, if we have to pay tolls. Anyway, if the new causey does for you, the steam machines will as likely do for us."

They rode on, not in complete silence, but deep in thought.

(And here Hudson's journal came to an end, though the volume had many blank pages to spare. Some time later, and in a quite different hand, someone else had written either by way of explanation or as an aide memoir: "Three runts lost Cross Keys Wash through thievery. Herd 571 at Bullock Hill. Prices recovered slightly but remained modest. Loss, after dues, over one pound per head." It was an unworthy epitaph).

More of Mr Hume's Reminiscences

Holt, Norfolk
Saturday, June 5, 1880

A DISTRESSING business all round. A very distressing business indeed. It is surely unnecessary for me to reaffirm that I love my wife dearly, and I am pleased to suspect that, if pressed to do so, she would return a similar happy sentiment, so that in many ways we are ideally suited and strive constantly to present this very picture to friends and relations who are often moved to remark on our outward serenity. Yet at the same time I feel there is some temperamental weakness about her which occasionally intrudes upon my constant striving for intellectual development. It is well known, of course, that the female does not possess the same level of development as the gentleman, being less able to grasp the intricacies of thought and debate in matters commercial or philosophical, or in the arts, and that is how it should be, for aside from our dear Queen, the Mother of the Nation, gentlewomen are in the main the better prepared and equipped for matters domestic and the chitter-chatter of the sitting-room. Yet I sometimes yearn for a greater understanding, on my dear wife's part, of the breadth and depth of my work and interests, and of the considerable intellectual effort that it demands.

All that apart, and much to my distaste, I find it necessary to record the passing of a quite unpleasant and uncomfortable night, this business of the cook having quite unbalanced everyone and banished all reason in the household, my dear wife herself appearing totally unable to understand that my decision yesterday to dismiss cook forthwith was, quite simply, the only correct and the only proper course of action open to me. For reasons of her own, which try as I might I have been quite unable to fathom, she chose to overlook the correctness of my decision and dwell instead upon the very great inconvenience the matter has doubtless thrust upon her. As a result I spent a wretched night in my study, sometimes reading Hudson's journal simply because of an inability to sleep, and for something to occupy my waking mind, and the rest of the dark hours endeavouring to sleep on the chaise longue. In the end I was awakened at some awful hour by a noise at the door, and rose, ill tempered and stiff of neck and hip, to find Emily standing there with the scuttle preparing to tend to the fire. She was evidently surprised to see me, and bobbed and apologised, but I shushed her and told her to proceed, drew the dark drapes to let in the light, and then stood by the window and watched as she busied herself around the grate.

Dear Emily. I truly believe she is the constant saviour of our household. She was quickly appraised of the situation and was even largely responsible for helping to heal the breach, for when she knocked later to inform me that breakfast was ready I entered the dining-room to find my dear wife there, too, a matter which I believe was entirely Emily's doing. In the event I breakfasted well, calling for coffee instead of my usual tea, and made all the usual conversations with my dear wife. Of course, I sensed there remained a certain coolness between us, largely on her part I must say, for I myself harboured absolutely no feelings of ill will, and we finally managed to plan the rest of our day, including preparations to find a replacement cook. In the meantime Emily once again came to our rescue, volunteering to do the kitchen work, including the cooking of some simple dishes, in addition to her other duties and until such time as a new cook is appointed. She is a jewel, this girl.

Otherwise, strangely out of sorts all day. Even a brisk walk through the town and past the bookshop, which has still not complied with my modest order, did not entirely banish the feelings of lethargy, but at least I resolved not to sleep in the study again, if I can possibly avoid it. I did, at the same time, reflect briefly on Hudson's journal, for having acquired it some years ago, and the contents having evaporated entirely from my mind, last night's re-reading brought it back fresh and new and whetted my interest once more. Resolved to pursue the business further.

And it was a curious business, the 1829 drove. It was totally out of character for Hudson to have failed so badly and to have incurred such catastrophic losses, and yet his journal does make plain many matters were out of his hands largely through the intervention of others, particularly the land agent, the evidently odious Mr Crawley.

Quite naturally, the end burden of financial loss was carried by Hudson, and because of his inability to fulfill his fiscal responsibilities then it was only right that the proper legal procedures should have been allowed to flow along their regal course. But even now, fifty years later, so many matters still seem unresolved. And so many fingers of suspicion appear to point in the same direction, and at the same possible culprit - the curious financial arrangement constructed by Crawley, within which the agent invested even more of Mr Porter's money; the non-arrival of any letter from Mr Porter to Hudson; the matter of the inadequate nailing and the cues which fell to ruin to the great harm of the herd; the attack on the drove; and the report of unsavoury parties awaiting the drove at Setchey. Alas, I do not even know what happened there, who Hudson met or what he did, for it seems to have been an episode wiped completely from the record.

But it was a curious business all round, which has left me pondering two other central concerns: what was in the bag thrust into Hudson's hand as he left the Shire Hall in disgrace in 1833, and who was it from; and if Crawley was responsible for most if not all of the ills which befell Hudson and the drove, what were his motives? It is abundantly plain Crawley was a rogue, so reason and calculated planning must have been behind his villainy.

A further question occurred to me as I strolled the last few yards home. What happened to Mr Porter in 1829 or 1830, or in any event in the years after the drove? Consumed with fascination I repaired immediately to my study, brushing aside an attempt by Emily, in the hallway, to deliver some trivial message or other, and searched the shelves for a particular 1845 Norfolk almanack. I checked the index and leafed through the pages, and there he was, in the section relating to Blakeney, at the head of the lists of Merchants and Maltsters, Master Mariners and Shoemakers, Carriers and Wheelwrights, under Farmers (and Owners): Porter, Aemilius. I closed the book and replaced it on the shelf.

So Mr Porter survived the scandal, at least for a few years, as did his farm. I had hoped, I suppose, for rapid resolution of this historical matter. Yet when I thought about it later I realised Mr Porter's financial survival, however fragile, actually muddied the waters even further.

Saturday, later that evening
My dear wife still somewhat frosty in her attitude towards me, so spent an interesting hour in the garden watching and advising Secker as he did a little digging and generally tidied the flower borders. We spoke of many things, including the war and the prospects for this year's grain prices. Secker unusually well informed in such matters, and decidedly despondent on the question of farming in Norfolk. All is not well, he claimed, and went on to say he had heard of tenant farmers and landowers, some well respected families among them, who are already in financial difficulty. What a business!

A little rain this pm, but a calm, quiet evening.

Sunday
Church as usual, and as usual we presented ourselves as a united and contented couple to our acquaintances, and to Brumell, who seemed out

of sorts. His sermon a weak soup of nothingness. Most unlike him. Dinner somewhat scant, though Emily had cooked a passable veal and ham pie, with hashed mutton and vegetables. It was clear by her attitude that my dear wife did not fully approve of the quality or the quantity, but she bravely bore her discontent and maintained her silence, retiring to her room immediately afterwards.

Thursday
Hurrah, hurrah! Ellis's man finally arrived with the volumes I had particularly requested, which at least alleviates me of the task of writing to him to revoke the order, for the shop took such an unusually long time. A few years ago the order would have been finalised with much greater expediency, but I suppose in these modern times we cannot expect things to work as well as they did. Ah! me. Unwrapping the parcel, I saw that Surtees' effort was a slim, green booklet of a type often produced by amateurs. But we shall see. I shall give it the benefit of my attention in due course.

Weather passably warm, so my dear wife and I have been able to take the air through the town on occasions, a recreation she professes to enjoy. Otherwise, she has said little these past few days, yet seems dedicated, I am glad to say, to the task of finally engaging a suitable new cook. In consequence, and despite the warmth and brightness of the weather, I have spent unusually long hours in my study, which I must say I enjoy, and have begun the monumental task of sorting through Cracknell's boxes of papers and files and through other collected detritus relating to the drove and to the main participants.

The scale of Hudson's demise quickly became apparent, and although I must have been aware of the situation at the time (it was, after all, half a century ago), it had quite slipped from the bounds my recollection. But it can be summarised thus. In 1829 the prices for runts were low to average at St Fay's Fair; Hudson's depleted herd lost money (as the footnote in his journal makes clear); and Hudson himself was charged with the entire burden of the loss. Because the law at that time did not allow drovers a facility to adopt bankruptcy proceedings, he lost everything, including his home and land at Hempstead. All his possessions were sold. Even then, some say, he was still not able to meet the complete debt. Mr Porter, as main creditor, lawfully received the largest portion of what funds there were, though it is clear he also lost a great deal of capital on the drove.

So it was not, as might have been thought, a combination of old age and the new-fangled railways that finished off Hudson as a drover - for it is plain he was a broken man, and never worked properly again - but unpaid bills. His reputation, like the business of long-distance droving, quite simply evaporated. As for his wife, she disappeared off the pages of history at this point and may even have left the district, though I know not where to. And as for Hudson, it is said he found lodging at a bush house somewhere near Thornage, living free in return for yard jobs, sleeping on straw next to a stable. I have little or no knowledge of what happened after that.

Monday the 14th
A quite beastly week-end. Brumell away yet again and some timid wretch scarce able to open his mouth took morning service. Then an inundation of my dear wife's friends and relations quite overwhelmed the household. Tea and sweetmeats, chitterings and cluckings and chatterings. Absolutely beastly. I left them to it at one point and wandered through the market place in order to clear my mind of the debris and effort of gossiping about everything and nothing.

Tuesday
Finally, an opportunity to examine Surtees' labour of love, printed by Smith of Soho Square in 1866, which is titled Julius Caesar: Did He Cross the Channel? The answer seems self evident to my mind, but we shall see. Am also intrigued as to the background of the author who is, according to the title page, the Rev Scott F Surtees who was, or possibly still is, rector of Sprotburgh parish in Yorkshire. Now I am of course slightly familar with the works of Robert Surtees, who was born of an old Durham family and died some 20 years ago. He was author of the splendidly successful Jorrocks' Jaunts and Jollities, and other tales of the hunter, hounds and the hunted, a volume which, acquaintances have told me, raises much wholesome laughter. I confess I do not know, as following the hounds is not an enthusiasm of mine. To be frank, I find horses smelly, muddy, unpredictable and entirely unendearing, and so have left the business alone and the matter of horses to others. Nevertheless, whether our ardent cleric is a member of the same Surtees family, a son even, I do not know. But I shall take a risk and label him as Surtees the Younger.

　　After a considerable perusal of the work I am less intrigued with the central thrust of his supposition, usefully paraphrased by the writer in his first paragraph thus: " . . . that Caesar never set foot at Boulogne or Calais, never crossed the Channel or set eyes on Dover or Deal, but that he sailed from some place in front of the mouths of the Rhine or Scheldt, most probably from a peninsular formerly the fore-shore of Walcheren, that he made the coast of Britain in his first expedition, off Cromer; that in his second he purposed to make the land at or near Wells, and being carried a little beyond the point, found himself off Hunstanton and, pulling in to the shore at Brancaster Bay, fixed his camp there."

Well, there is much food for thought here! But Surtees the Younger goes further. Not only did Caesar sail past Cromer, he writes, where native warriors hurled their spears at the passing ships from the top of the cliffs, but on the second expedition came ashore at Brancaster, where there is the remains of a Roman camp, and then made a night march of some twelve miles to Hanworth, where he met the enemy by the river.

Surtees the Younger then proposes a chain of Roman military forts, including Holme, which seems dubious to me, and most ridiculously, Holkham, which I have always supposed, and which most educated thinkers suppose, is either Danish or English in origin. Even so, the author insists on marking out Holkham as Caesar's advanced camp and Hanworth as the stronghold of the British Celts. One day, as Surtees the Younger himself concludes his epic commentary, truth will come uppermost and error disappear. In the meantime, I draw no pleasure from such nonsense.

Later

A new cook appointed. Introduced to me, I found her somewhat surly and unpleasant, but my dear wife greatly relieved and bouyant about the business, so I shall say no more on the subject.

June the 16th

This afternoon, at last an opportunity to retrieve my version of Hudson's 1833 appearance before the Justices, and to copy the review findings into my commonplace book. Clearly, Hudson was seeking a settlement ruling in Holt in order to claim relief, his condition since the drove of 1829 having evidently become more and more difficult. The document (and I can vouch for its accuracy for I took it from the original record many years ago) reads:

"Examination of Thomas Hudson, labourer, before Mr JW Tomlinson and Mr WE Girdlestone, at the Shire Hall, Holt, dated September, 1833. Who saith he is about 53 years of age, having been born in Chertsey in Surrey of lawful parents. That he continued to reside with his parents, working as a cattle driver, until he lawfully married Elizabeth Holding of Chertsey, there being no children. That in 1816 he and his wife moved to Hempstead, Norfolk, where he was a land labourer, and that three years later he turned to his former profession, that of drover, being familiar with the business and confident of contractual arrangements with leading farmers and landowners of the area. That for ten years he was very successful in his profession, bringing many droves from Galloway to Norfolk for the St Faith's Fair. That in 1829 there was an unsuccessful drove for Mr Aemilius Porter of Blakeney, following which he was unable to meet his financial obligations, and that he did lose his home, chattels and land in the payment of debt, some of which was not met. That his wife subsequently left the county, he does not know where, and that he lodged for a time with a Mrs Charles of Thornage where he did yard work but received no wage but a roof and his keep. That in March this year following the death of Mrs Charles, and the new owner of the property not wishing to continue the arrangement, he returned to the parish of Holt in order to seek employment, but finding none, has been sleeping in empty buildings and stables and finding food where he can, and is now applying for settlement in order to obtain relief and other assistance to help him to find work." Beneath that, on the original document, and written in a quite different hand and in a jocular manner, on the right hand margin, was the statement: "Rejected (by the Justices). Settlement to be sought in Chertsey." The writer had surrounded his statement with elaborate curlicules.

Having just completed the transcription of this document into my book I must confess to taking at least a few moments of quiet reflection, to a brief period of sadness, for it was my understanding at the time, and remains so even now, that Hudson was a man of many considerable qualities, of honour and respect and standing; and yet a man treated harshly by circumstance and, I will allow, by historical memory; for it is these records which will remain alive, and not the esteem in which he was held, which will be forgotten and which, save for two or three of us in Holt has already been quite obliterated from memory by the passage of time. Of course, it is abundantly clear he was properly dealt with by the law as it stood at that particular moment, which was right, but I thank God that in these modern and enlightened times our Poor receive a much improved level of sympathetic benefaction. Poor Hudson, whose plea for assistance was so abruptly dismissed by the Justices; who had a bag of something or other thrust into his hand by a boy as the crowd milled about him immediately after the hearing; who thereafter appeared to gain the means of ekeing out a meagre living for a year or two; who died quite alone and deserted in 1837, when he was 57; and who was buried in an unmarked grave which neither I, nor even Brumell for that matter, can any longer locate. All is humility!

June 18, being a Friday
What a business, what a thoroughly distressing business! Having only recently and successfully circumnavigated an irritating little difficulty relating to the previous cook and the appointment of her replacement (dreadful woman!), we now have two further matters of distressing content which, once again, can only disturb the delicate balance of my dear wife's general health and demeanour.

First, our dear Emily, who has been with us for the last eight years, since she was a mere child, and whom we have watched grow and have nurtured almost as one of our own, has now become wretchedly sad, constantly strained, and prone to outbursts of tearfulness. My dear wife is beside herself with consternation and worry, and more than once has raised the question of whether she ought to dismiss her, but I have counselled patience in this matter, believing it to be a female malady which will pass in the goodness of time. I sincerely hope so, for recently Emily has been quite cutting in her manner and conversation, even to me.

That is one matter. The other arrived yesterday afternoon, by letter, a communication from solicitors in chambers in Old Bank of England Court, Norwich, bringing distressing tidings of the sudden and unexpected death of my dear wife's aunt whom we had the very great pleasure of visiting in Pottergate, also in Norwich, on the occasion of our foray only last month. My dear wife, quite distraught at the news, retired to her room instantly. What made the matter considerably worse was the realisation that the dear lady died some two weeks' ago, and thus only two weeks after our visit, and that because no one saw fit to communicate the matter to us at the time the funeral has already been held.

Further, the letter said my dear wife's aunt, no doubt in recognition of the love and affection shared between them, had bequeathed her some relatively small costume trifle or other, with the bulk of the estate, including the value of the Pottergate property, going to a distant relative currently residing in Nottingham. However, the letter continued, the matter was likely to be contested by the aunt's companion, who we also met, on the grounds that the will was drawn up over two decades ago and thus made no recognition of the fact that she, the companion, had lived with her and had nursed her these last eight years.

It seems to me the impertinence of the companion knows no bounds. I am not aware that she is a member of aunt's loving family, or that she has any claim whatsoever to any portion of the estate, but we can only wait and see and allow the majesty of the law to run its course.

Evening
My dear wife still consumed with grief and confined to her room. I particularly asked Emily to attend to her, and to tread respectfully and quietly in the vicinity of my dear wife's room, as she is grieving, and was rather shocked when Emily retorted, "What a lark!" or some such thing, and stalked off. I am quite at a loss to understand what has got into the girl.

Saturday
After breakfast, persuaded my dear wife of the need to partake of fresh air, and of the importance of taking her mind off the affair of her late lamented aunt, just for a short time, and she finally agreed to accompany me on a jaunt on condition I understood she was too upset and distressed to make constant cheerful conversation. I accepted her condition, such as it was. In the end, and after some discussion as to where we should make our visit, the ostler's lad drove us to Booton, there to view the latest changes Whitwell Elvin is making to St Michael and All Angels. We had hoped to see him, but a labourer said to me he had gone to Norwich on some errand or other.

Otherwise a topping day, with masons, joiners, glaziers, rubble and materials all over the place, making it quite difficult to attend to the church itself. It is an extraordinary business, for Elvin is encasing the entire building behind new walls, and adding a baptistry and a vestry. Some say he is also planning to add two somewhat feeble towers and even some sort of minaret construction. But we shall see. Perhaps caution will finally prevail. Even so, I fear Brumell will be aghast at the audacity of it all.

Monday, June the 21st
Two quite curious incidents today. In the first, during mid-morning and being aware that Emily had completed her breakfast duties, and my dear wife being otherwise engaged on some gentle activity or other, I called her to my study to help me sort Cracknell's papers from the bank boxes. However, the girl seemed so unusually quiet and so distracted that on two occasions I was prevailed upon to speak to her quite sharply, fearing that she was not concentrating on her task. On one occasion I thought I saw tears, or the beginning of tears, upon her face, but she turned away from me and brushed a hand over her eyes so that when she turned back to resume her work I was not certain that I had noticed the matter properly, and so said nothing.

In the event we did, after some time and with considerable difficulty, complete the task, and I was predisposed to thank her profusely for her efforts in an attempt, I suppose, to bring a little light into her mysterious darkness, but she said nothing, turned abruptly and fled from the room. A strange business. Nevertheless, the papers from Cracknell's boxes are now ranged across every available flat surface in my study, save for the floor, so that I can move easily and freely from one pile to another and compare one with another. Correspondence, memoranda, legal documents tied into rolls with ribbon, legal documents untied, financial statements, counter foils, credit lists, counter notes and the like, and other banking ephemera. As yet each pile is not in order according to its date, but that shall be my next task, earliest at the top and latest at the bottom, so that I may begin to read the documents in proper order and thus gain some sense of the episode. It will undoubtedly take me a long time and I decided, before lunch, that I would begin the task in a day or two, my mind being too distracted for study by the present unusual demeanour of Emily.

Which brings me to the second curious incident of the day. Early in the afternoon, my dear wife having retired for a sleep, I settled in my chair in the study, preparing to read Surtees' nonsensical commentary again (for I am quite prepared to allow him time to convince me of the central core of his argument, though I allow it is most unlikely he will succeed), when there was a clamour in the domestic area downstairs, the clang of a metal utensil as it fell to the stone floor, and the sound of cook's voice demanding, "Enough, enough. That is quite enough."

Utterly perplexed at this disturbance, and hearing the outside door open and close with some rapidity, I was persuaded to rise from my chair, walk to the window, and view the scene in the square below.

There was little to be seen save the usual passers-by, and no obvious reason for a disturbance, and I was about to turn away from the window and return to my chair, Surtees' little volume in hand, when I noticed a youth leaning quite insolently and expectantly on the other side of Fish Hill beside the corner of the old costumiers' shop. He was looking in my direction, or rather, towards the front door, or the passage beside the house, and even though there seemed something faintly familiar about him I could make no proper identification because of the cap he had pulled low over his face. Then I heard the front door open and close again and watched as Emily - for it was she - walked briskly towards the lad, and when she reached him, instead of remonstrating with him for some misdemeanour or other, or whatever activity it was that so distracted cook, she took him by the elbow and ushered him around the far corner of the shop so they were no longer in full view of myself or anyone else in the house who might have been looking out. I was flabbergasted! A full minute later Emily, looking somewhat bothered and distracted, and walking quickly, walked alone back to the house and closed the front door. The youth did not appear again.

Only later did I learn the true events of the entire episode, and it was my dear wife, who had been disturbed by the noise during her afternoon retirement, who garnered most of the detail. Apparently Emily had been in a difficult frame of mind all day and finally confessed to cook that she had been "walking out" for two weeks and that there had been some sort of disagreement. All that day, apparently, the youth concerned had been standing outside the house hoping to see Emily, in order to speak to her, a fact of which Emily was quite aware and of which she was talking incessantly to cook, whose patience, being short, and who in any event was busily preparing the forthcoming meal, finally demanded the girl be quiet on the subject. At this, and no doubt realising she had overstepped the line of propriety, Emily rushed from the house to confront the youth and to demand that he leave the vicinity and not disturb her until she had completed her duties, which was when I saw her cross the hill.

Everything is quiet again now, as I write, but am resolved to speak to Emily about this patent silliness.

My dear wife also told me at dinner, after Emily had finished serving and had left the room, that the youth was in fact the ostler's boy, which surprised me greatly as I was under the impression she did not care for him, and that he had been seen loitering outside the house on several occasions during the previous week. It seems to me it was an episode which underlined once again the quite unrestrained attitudes of today's young generation, who would appear to know little of decorum and etiquette. I recall also the sight of bicyclists in Holt, and of a female (for I shall refrain from calling her a lady) smoking in the street. I suspect that today's youngsters do not have the mettle of our generation. But we shall see.

Thursday the 24th

We are experiencing a dry period of a sort that perenially spells difficulty in the garden, our well drained soils becoming very dusty almost overnight. Many of the flowers are beginning to wilt and there is the first sign of a discoloured patch in the centre of the lawn. Having mentioned the dryness of the garden in passing, my dear wife remarked over breakfast that perhaps Secker should be called in order to do something about it. Privately, I do not see what Secker can possibly do, unless he has a means, unknown to me, of making it rain.

Meanwhile, I am happy to record progress of sorts in the matter of Hudson, and Cracknell's boxes of bank papers, for a cursory glance at a few of them, while awaiting this evening's call to dinner, immediately convinced me that Crawley had his tentacles on Mr Porter's private affairs and private money to a quite surprising degree. There are letters from Crawley to the bank requesting withdrawals on Mr Porter's behalf and at his apparent behest, and even letters from Mr Porter to the bank, or rather to the assistant bank manager, a Mr Rennie, authorising Mr Crawley to act on his behalf in matters financial. This has come as a surprise to me as I had always imagined Mr Porter to be a solid, earthy farmer with a wide knowledge of the world and certainly someone in full possession of all his faculties. Perhaps he was not, though, for these notes and papers demonstrate a degree of gullibility astonishing even at this distance in time from the actual event.

Friday
Strolling by the church I happened across Brumell who was in a most expansive and friendly mood and clearly amenable to conversation, and so because of the heat we entered the coolness of the church and sat on our usual pew near the font. He told me Fiddy had been to see him again and that the man would not allow the carstone question to rest, and further, that he, Fiddy, intended to begin a correspondence with the editor of the Eastern Daily Press of Norwich putting forward his theory that the earlier church had been built of carstone and that what we see in the tower are fragments from this earlier church. I told Brumell the matter was beyond my comprehension and that Fiddy's theory was unproveable, save for excavation on a considerable scale, but that I would consider a suitable reply in print only after a letter from Fiddy had appeared in the newspaper columns. Brumell also counselled patience, said he had resolved to remain a neutral in the matter, and expressed hope the disagreement would not cause discontent among the congregation. I replied that I would never resort to such a crude device as outspoken argumentation, as he well knew, but pointed out that Fiddy could sometimes present a disagreeable picture of himself; at which Brumell raised his hands in mock horror and said, "Oh, peace, peace!"

Then our conversation drifted once again on to the question of memory and change, matters we had discussed briefly some weeks before, and I expressed the view that Mr Darwin and the evolutionists had to an extent underlined the point that change was a natural occurrence, whereupon Brumell interjected that Darwin, for all his powers of thought and reasoning, had quite failed to allocate a sufficiently large or influential role for God in the entire process, and that the whole scientific matter was still very much called into question, particularly by churchmen.

I then expressed an idea which had come to me some time after our first conversation on the subject, namely, that the process of memory was also, in part, a preparation for death, a thought which evidently left Brumell driven high and dry on the wide shores of misunderstanding. So I explained my idea further. Memory, I suggested, was also a means of introducing world weariness, a longing for something more, a recognition that change has occurred and that, as one grows older, the world one has known has dissolved and is gradually disappearing. Brumell merely repeated his earlier point that only God's love is unchanging and everlasting, a sentiment with which I heartily concurred, of course, but it does seem to me that those who cannot respond to change, who cannot themselves evolve, risk oblivion.

Evening
Happy to record that of late Emily seems much chastened after all the
unseemly goings on, and grateful to be remaining with us.

Tuesday, July 20
Idleness is a mortal sin, and am much chastened by the sudden realisation
I have written next to nothing in my commonplace book for some time. I
plead lethargy. The hot weather has continued unbroken, most of my days
being spent with a book sitting under the fruit trees or consoling my dear
wife, who is much distressed by the incessant heat. At one point I suggested that perhaps an expedition to Cromer and a bathe in the sea would
be beneficial, but she maintained she was too ill and exhausted to be able
to undertake such a tiresome journey. How cook manages in the kitchen I
do not know, for the place, I noticed today, has the temperature of a fur-
nace, mainly from the fire in the range.

Friday, 23rd
Cooler today. Able to undertake a little work in my study and so spend
further time with the Cracknell papers. Came across an invoice from
Crawley for the cost of the 1829 rental of a house called The Lodge at
Durisdeer, Galloway, with servants and retainers, for one month, at what
seems to me to have been an exhorbitant price. A handwritten note said
the taking of the house was for a "business venture." Also according to the
invoice, which bore signatures, the sum was paid, interestingly, by Rennie
out of Mr Porter's account. My suspicious nature leads me to suspect that
this Mr Rennie may also have been involved in Crawley's little "business
venture," but time will tell. There are many piles of paper still unexamined,
some of them, I note, private memoranda and jottings.

Tuesday, August 3
Much excitement and gloom in town when news was received of a further
setback in Afghanistan. This time General Burrows' brigade of 3000 has
been defeated, with barely 1000 brave men escaping. They say the city of
Maiwand is lost, and also the garrison therein, but that Roberts is soon to
march to Kandahar with 10,000 troops to put matters right. It is a worrying business, for nothing seems to be going right, militarily, at the moment. Either our boys lack the patriotic spark of my or earlier generations
or there is too much indiscipline and not enough preparation. I confess I
am confused, for our generals seem such splendid fellows.

Weather cooler and altogether more pleasant, the recent showers having
had the effect of freshening things considerably. Cook and Emily have been
skinning and stoning the Imperatrice plums and beginning the process of

preserving them, creating charming domestic scenes. Cook seems much less surly than hitherto, though her tongue, I have noticed, retains its sharpness.

Wednesday, August 11
Life is maintaining the even tenor of a typically sultry summer, interspersed with occasional showers, reflecting, I suppose, the daily outlook of our little family in Bull Street. Delight this morning, however, as I uncovered from Cracknell's memoranda pile a short biographical note, presumably sketched at a time when Crawley was having monetary dealings with the bank, adding marginally to the small store of information I already have about him.

It at least confirmed that Jonathan Crawley originally hailed from Richmond (family background unknown); that he received an education of sorts; that as a young man he worked at various lowly professions with no discernible success or distinction; and that in the early 1820s he moved to a foundry at Darlington, whereupon he suddenly professed to have become an engineer. There is no indication of apprenticeship, marriage or children, but there is an implied indication that Mr Crawley took upon himself more airs and graces and responsibility than even his shoulders could carry, that he left the foundry abruptly (reasons unknown), that he seems to have set himself up as some sort of agent (the bank paper says simply "an agent," as though the reader, or the bank staff, ought to know), evidently familiarising himself with a number of aspects of trade. Then in 1826 he turned up in Norfolk and by 1827 was installed as Mr Porter's farm agent, or secretary, at Blakeney. And that is more or less all the information the memorandum contained, which leaves, in my own mind at least, a lingering doubt as to the man's basic integrity and honesty, though it is certain that in this I have been greatly influenced by Hudson's journal of the drove. Crawley was not a particularly nice or a particularly trustworthy man, that is plain.

Sunday
Took advantage of the warm though somewhat milder weather to enjoy a short perambulation to Bayfield, having first made certain we would not be driven by the ostler's boy, for I will not have Emily disturbed again. This time our driver was an elderly man, one Towler, who in his youth was a famed hell-raiser but who did badly as a soldier, so I am told, and now lives with various unsavoury females and assorted children. My dear wife quite rightly raised the question of morals when I mentioned to her that Towler was our man, and asked whether it was right we should be seen to be employing him, but I assured her that he was now an old man

of very few words who in public, anyway, kept himself to himself, and she eventually accepted my choice. In fact Ballachey, who is most punctilious in such matters, had told me earlier that Towler, despite his background, was trustworthy, and a good driver. And so it proved. We rode to Bayfield smoothly, and in silence.

Part of our journey was an official visitation to acquaintances, by name Proudfoot, who live on the edge of the heath, and we were made splendidly welcome and were most engagingly entertained. It was during this visit that the lady of the house, a particular social acquaintance of my dear wife, informed us that their eldest daughter, who is somewhat plain and has inherited a number of unfortunate mannerisms, was to marry next spring a man in commerce in Fakenham, and that entire family would be delighted were we to find ourselves able to attend. We also expressed delight in the matter, of course, and said we would consider it more formally when the invitation was received, though intimating our possible acceptance. I have to confess that, afterwards, the prospect of attending such a wedding filled me with gloom and for some reason darkened the remainder of the excursion.

Towler also took us home and saw to the pony and the cart, and said nothing the entire time, so that a journey which had begun in sunshine and such high spirits ended, as far as I was concerned, under a large cloud of melancholy, even though my dear wife is already considering what she would need to wear at the church and even planning a shopping expedition to Norwich. Women are prepostrous creatures, seemingly sent into paradoxisms of delight at the thought of a piece of flummery or the sight of a bunch of ribbons. Goodness, how we men suffer when we are made to listen to it all!

My dear wife has also announced she and others are to hold regular playing-card parties, which means I shall be able to spend more time in my study.

Emily seemingly quite spirited and gay at the moment.

Roses require a great deal of watering, and Secker concerned as to the browning of the lawns. It has been a quite difficult gardening year.

Friday, August 20
A monumental day of an absolutely champion sort, for I have discovered what was behind the mysterious delivery of a small bag to Hudson the moment he left the Shire Hall hearing in 1833, and more over, the name of the person behind it. It happened like this. I had been puzzling over the role of Rennie, the assistant bank manager over the period of the drove, and had already noted from the many bank documents etc that his signature did not seem to appear on anything at all after 1829. It was as though,

in 1829, Rennie vanished from the face of the earth, or at least, left the bank's employ.

Whether or not that is so I am still not certain, and it is a small matter in this particular story, though significant, nonetheless. Rennie seems to have been the person who dealt with Crawley in matters of the farm and, in consequence, the drove, and who, quite naturally, also dealt with the financial affairs of Mr Porter. It had already crossed my mind that Crawley and Rennie might have been involved together in some sort of fraud, for the bank official and the land agent were unusually well placed to interfere in such matters, and between them they had a great deal of information about Mr Porter's holdings and affairs. Then I dismissed the notion. What could they possibly have gained? Porter's agricultural affairs, if not in a parlous state in 1828/29, were fragile, to say the least. It would not have taken much to have tipped him into bankruptcy, in which case there would have been no capital, which would have been taken by creditors, and no land, which would have been sold. What could they have gained?

Anyway, I was attempting to verify the fact that Rennie's signature, and thus his presence at the bank, appeared to end after 1829, and was searching through all manner of papers and trivia, when I came across a cash receipt made out in the name of Mr Turnbull, who was the bank manager and thus Rennie's superior, for the sum of fifty pounds. He had evidently drawn it from bank funds for his own unspecified use. The receipt was dated September the 7, 1833. A careful perusal of the bank's main accounts ledger of the time showed the dealing had been properly entered and accounted, so that at least it was lawful and above board. Now, in itself this receipt meant absolutely nothing. The bank manager, Turnbull, might have required the money for any number of reasons connected with the smooth running of the bank, for example, to pay staff or trade accounts, even the coalman who kept the bank's fires burning in winter. And this I would have believed had it not been for a slight unpremeditated movement on my part. Quite without thinking, and without knowning why, I turned the receipt over, and there, written in what appeared to be Turnbull's own hand (for it corresponded with his signature on the front of the receipt, and looked to have been written at the same time), were the words, "To Hudson, for the Rennie affair."

Thus it became clear it was Turnbull, the manager of the bank, who interceded immediately after the judicial hearing and who seems to have given Hudson sufficient money to have allowed him to live modestly, if not comfortably, for the next two or three years. But again, why? And why hand it over publicly, when it would certainly have provoked public comment? The only tentative conclusions I can reach at the moment are that it was an attempt to buy off Hudson, to try to persuade him not to bring into the public domain any whiff of scandal about Rennie, which would have seriously damaged the reputation of the bank, and that the payment was made not so much in public but immediately after the judicial verdict which refused Hudson settlement, so that Hudson had no time to sit and consider his woes but could jingle his coins and know that he could at least find a roof, and not starve, and thus escape the workhouse for a little longer.

They are ill discoverers that think there is no land,
when they can see nothing but the sea.
(Francis Bacon, 1561-1626, Advancement of Learning)
Indeed!

Thursday, August 26
A singular business today. Two mornings ago Harcourt called at the tradesman's door - the man has few pretensions to social station - with yet another bag brim full of bits and pieces picked up during hours of solitary wanderings on his fields, and as usual Emily took them into the scullery, prior to washing them. On this occasion, however, and being distracted by some other detail of her daily business, she forgot all about them and cook, finding the bag later and not knowing what it was or what it contained, even if she did look inside, pushed it into some corner or other and promptly forgot all about it, too. I knew Harcourt had called, for I had heard his voice in the street through my open window, and naturally presumed Emily would appear with the man's contribution to civilised knowledge later in the afternoon, after the pieces had been washed. But nothing appeared, and it was not until yesterday that I remembered to mention the matter to Emily, who flushed prettily at her forgetfulness and rushed to the scullery to retrieve the same.

An hour later, when she returned to my study with the artefacts and spread them before me on my desk, they were still wet from her washing of them under the pump to rid them of soil and debris, and droplets of water fell on the polished surface. Poor distracted Emily! Already flustered and apologetic for having forgotten the bag, she was now anguished by the thought of damage to my polished desk and scurried away to fetch cleaning rags to wipe away the mess. I told her not to worry, and dismissed the matter as lightly as I could.

Emily also produced a short note from Harcourt which she had found in the bag, in which he explained he had only recently been able to resume his wanderings now that the harvest had been gathered and the plough teams had departed. Only later did I glance with any degree of concentration at the artefacts scattered in front of me, and only then did I feel astonishment at what the man had found. I picked them over carefully, and examined them one by one.

There were three small lumps of some material which is unknown to me, though possibly plaster, one of them bearing traces of colouring; three fragments of pre-Roman worked flint, of quite exquisite design and with edges still sharp, even today; and the rest plainly Roman. A good deal of it, too. Two coins, badly corroded and sorely affected by their long sojourn under ground, so that I could not identify or date them; pieces of roof tiling; fragments of some clay conduit or other; several pieces of green glass, which might have emanated from the same jar or vessel, so close was the colouration; fragments of familiar grey kitchenware, and two items of good quality Samian ware; the inevitable oyster shell fragments; and five more pieces of tessera.

My immediate conclusions were two-fold. First, that the collection, and the others brought in by Harcourt, indicate Roman buildings, possibly a villa, somewhere in the vicinity of his holding, and second, and particularly as Harcourt's note also relayed the information that there were more artefacts to come, that the Roman population of the area was probably much more dense than I or anyone else had supposed.

They seem to have been everywhere! So much so that I immediately began to reconstruct in my mind a theory which had occurred to me some years ago, relating to the earthworks at Warham All Saints, which I visited last year and which prevailing fashion labels as Danish. My thought then was that the camp is surely much earlier than Danish, and is more likely Roman or even early English. Now, and seeing the spread of Roman artefacts and the degree to which the Roman seems to have settled this area, I am inclined to believe I was correct.

Surtees comes to mind, of course, with his fanciful theory of the Caesarian invasions and the construction of Warham as one of his strongholds in the war against the tribes. But that is nonsense. Although difficult to perceive entirely in one glance because of tree growth in the centre and because someone, presumably the Holkham Estate, cut a slice from one of the earthen embankments a century ago, to the evident benefit of the Stiffkey river, Warham strikes me as having a defensive purpose. It is plainly too large and too complicated a place to have been built by an invasion force, unless it was planning to stay a long time in the area, which it was not. But we shall see. In the meantime, I have written to Harcourt to thank him for his continued efforts and to say I would like to visit the location of his perambulations one day, simply to see the lie of the land.

Early September
Have been reading Cracknell's papers and found one of particular interest, an early bank reference relating to Crawley which mentioned that he, Crawley, was a supporter of the steam railway movement, having been most impressed by, and I quote, "the Darlington demonstration, September, 1825."

Friday, September 17
Oh! dear. What a business! It does seem to me the news these days is one thing after another, and I for one will be pleased to see the end of this year of 1880 which has brought us little but bad tidings and constant unsettlement. The present matter is this. A Norwich weekly newspaper of a quite scandalous nature, titled for some uncomprehensible reason, Daylight, has been attacking Brumell's friend Benjamin Armstrong, incumbent at East Dereham, for what it describes as his "Romish" leanings, an accusation which Mr Armstrong himself has naturally seen fit to deny on numerous occasions. On hearing of the latest publicity - for I could not bring myself to actually purchase a copy of Daylight - I hurried to see Brumell, to express my indignation, for I knew he would be sorely affected by the matter and distressed by the nature of the accusations, as indeed he was, adding that Mr Armstrong himself had told him some time ago he intended to travel to Norwich to confront the editor of this dreadful publication over the basis of these spurious claims.

  Altogether, a distressing affair. I know there are those with a great dread of Popery and Puseyism, who also distrust the High Church party, but Brumell assures me Mr Armstrong stays firmly on the side of right and even includes many contented dissenters among his congregation. These newspaper people have much to answer for.

Saturday
A thought has just occurred to me. Perhaps there was more to this railway business than meets the eye. If Crawley was indeed at Skerne Bridge in 1825 to see the railway, just as Hudson was four years later, and if he really was an engineer, then why did he leave the area shortly afterwards and head towards Norfolk? Perhaps this whole business has something to do with the railways. Am resolved to read up the matter further and to pursue it to a conclusion among the bank's papers.

Monday, September 27
While it would not be correct to state categorically that war has broken out within our little household, it would be accurate to say there is little peace. Indeed, artillery fire and isolated sniping has been noisy and persistent all

the wretched week-end. The whole business began on Saturday evening when we were at dinner. I had noticed, as I am sure had my dear wife, that Emily was not her self again, being tight-lipped and silent and somewhat abrupt in her manner. My patience at an end, I was preparing to admonish her, as I felt it was my duty to do, but my dear wife, in her compassion, signalled to me to it was better to remain silent, implying by her manner that staffing problems were her responsibility and that she would deal with the matter.

The meal - tapioca soup, steak and kidney pie, cold port, mashed potatoes and pickles, and baked lemon pudding - was passably interesting, though our new cook (dreadful woman) rarely excites my palate these days, but any semblance of conviviality was utterly destroyed when we finally reached the dessert stage. Emily placed the dishes on the table sharply and carelessly, and with a bit of a bang, provoking my dear wife said, "Really, Emily . . ." or some such thing, whereupon Emily, the poor dear girl, burst into floods of tears and rushed speedily from the room.

Of course, I was shocked beyond words at the girl's rudeness, but mindful of my dear wife's determination to manage these matters, decided to do nothing but continue my meal. Soon afterwards we heard the clatter of footsteps above us followed by the slam of Emily's door, and then the murmer of voices and the sound of more crying. Before my dear wife and I had completed the dessert, cook came in, apologetically, to report that Emily was not feeling well and that she had sent her to bed, which was just as well. The meal was ruined, the whole business being simply too distressing for my digestion.

Sometime later, and perceiving that cook had taken over Emily's duties, I asked her to bring coffee and brandy (for although quite aware of the evils of drink, I am also alive to the medicinal benefits of an occasional libation) to the sitting-room, and my dear wife and I sat for a time in silent contemplation of the problem. After a while my dear wife resolved to investigate the business for herself, and she left the sitting-room to speak first to cook and then to Emily in her room. When she returned, as I was savouring the brandy, she said, "Emily is not well. She is unwell." When I suggested we ought to send for the doctor, she said, "No, that is not necessary," rather sharply, I thought. In any event she would have none of it, implying that Emily would heal herself in the course of time.

Yesterday, Emily remained in her room, with cook handling the increased burden of work as best she could. Suggested to my dear wife we send the ostler's boy with a note for Emily's mother, but once again my dear wife said it was not necessary. It is a most vexing business. What is the matter with the girl? Am constantly perplexed by the vagaries of the female character.

Wednesday
Emily seemingly recovered and about her usual business again. When I
asked if all was well once more she blushed crimson and turned away.
What a charming, tiresome girl she is!

October 1, being a Friday
Took a long perambulation around the town and noticed a real feel of
autumn afoot. Damp air, dead leaves, skeletal trees, and a pinch of cold.
Later, soon after I returned home to sit before the fire, a wind arose, and I
could hear dead leaves swirling in the street outside.

Drive my dead thoughts over the universe
Like withered leaves to quicken a new birth!
And, by the incantation of this verse,
Scatter, as from an unextinguished hearth
Ashes and sparks, my words among mankind!
Be through my lips to unawakened earth
The trumpet of a prophecy! O, Wind,
If Winter comes, can Spring be far behind?
(Percy Bysshe Shelley, 1792-1822, Ode to the West Wind)

Monday, October 4
Strolled to church this morning as I wanted to discuss yesterday's sermon
with Brumell. Bitterly cold with a brisk, ill wind sweeping across the market place. Gave coin to boy in very poor clothes lurking on Fish Hill and
sheltering as best he could from the breeze. I was well wrapped, but this
was no thanks to Emily, who takes little interest in me these days, and
indeed, I suspect goes out of her way to avoid seeing me. Perhaps that is
my imagination, however.
   Brumell was talking to old Mrs Savory when I arrived, presumably about
the church flowers, and there seemed to be some sort of a minor dispute
for I noticed Brumell raise his eyebrows once or twice, and when Mrs Savory
finally turned away towards the main door she had a scowl which would
have done credit to a gargoyle. I sat down in our usual pew near the font,
and directly Mrs Savory had departed Brumell joined me. He dismissed
the altercation as a minor pebble on the stony path of life, and indeed (for
his kindness is, above all, his blessing) described Mrs Savory as a devoted
and tireless worker for the church.
   "If only there were more of them," he said, throwing his arms in the air
in the French manner.

Taking this as meaning that I, too, ought to be seen doing more, I put in an immediate riposte that my studies, allied to general exhaustion brought about by advancing years prevented me from pouring more energies into the church, but he assured me that this was not what he was inferring and that my regular donations to funds were a splendid and sufficient sign of my devotion. Somewhat gingerly, we left the matter thus. Instead, I gently chided him over what I considered a rather poor sermon on the yesterday during which he had again queried the role of our brave soldiers abroad, suggesting our politicians ought to look at the matter again and act with certainty and dynamism, all of which I interpreted as defeatist nonsense, and I told him I would have none of it.

Brumell replied that he was certainly not defeatist and would back our boys to the utmost, but he had occasional doubts as to the overall effectiveness of our campaigns and to the long-term aims of the enterprise. Brumell is a naive fellow sometimes, but I refrained from saying so for the sake of expediency.

Then he told me his friend Armstrong, of East Dereham, had visited Norwich and confronted the editor of Daylight in his office, and that the wretched man had finally apologised for that newspaper's indiscretions. Also, that Fiddy had brought him the draft of a letter on the church carstone question which he, Fiddy, intended to submit to the editor of the Daily Press of Norwich.

"Fiddy rakes over the same soil," Brumell said wearily, asking if I thought it worth while seeing Fiddy to try to persuade him away from his intended course of action. But I said no. The man had to put his ideas into print before I could begin to demolish them.

He also asked me if I had made progress on the Hudson mystery, and I was able to inform him I thought I had identified the core matter behind what was obviously an attempted fraud.

"And what was that?" Brumell asked.

"It was locomotion," I replied, deliberately mysteriously. "The triple curse of steam, progress and profit. But locomotion was at the heart of it."

To my very great glee, Brumell expressed total puzzlement.

Thursday, October 14

Shocking news, and the streets abuzz with excitement. The Transvaal has had the audacity to declare independence from Britain. What can this mean? Another war? While there are some who say we should not have annexed it purely for commercial gain in the first instance, a majority, I am sure, will see this latest business as a serious affront to our flag and our Queen. My dear wife was quite distressed at the news, and at the sounds of noisy crowds in the streets, and took to her room, and for a long time had Emily rushing upstairs and downstairs making and carrying various potions and vapours, ostensibly to relieve the anxiety. How this will help to redeem the situation I do not know. The crowds, in the main reasonably behaved, wandered up and down the market place for a long time, and it was early afternoon before the place fell quiet and one felt safe to go out.

My gardener Secker came this pm and began planting out the new roses which I had ordered. Advised him as to planting methods and the best position in which to place them. He said we needed to protect everything from persistent frosts, saying he believed there would be a deal of snow after Christmas and some very cold weather. I asked him how he knew, but he replied merely that the countryside and wildlife told him so. The matter is a mystery to me, but I hold that some of these country fellows do know what they are talking about.

Conversing further with him, Secker made the astonishing point that if war came then it would be of great assistance to the distressed state of local agriculture and bring considerable profit to industry and commerce, a point of view I found quite shocking, and told him so, arguing that surely commerce and industry would do everything they could to bring help and succour to our soldiers in whatever task they are called upon to perform.

"That is precisely what I mean," he said with a wry smile on his face.

Secker is a decent man, but sometimes too full of his own opinions. I sometimes despair of him, but he is a willing worker in the garden, given the right direction.

Wednesday
Paid Ellis's account for the books and ordered two more titles on aspects of archaeology which I will need if I am to write about Harcourt's land, the supposed villa, and whether or not the Danish Camp at Warham All Saints is Roman or even earlier. However, cannot get the Hudson business out of my mind, and I am determined to pursue it further early in the New Year. In the meantime, Cracknell's papers are taking over my study, carpeting every available surface and, at the last, a considerable percentage of the floor. Have ordered they must be left undisturbed, and even Emily no longer complains about the untidiness; then again, she says very little these days.

After lunch the post boy brought a letter with a Norwich postmark for my dear wife which turned out to be from the solicitors in Old Bank of England Court handling the affairs of her aunt, recently deceased, bringing news that the legal challenge to the Will had been dropped and that matters would now proceed in the prescribed, orderly manner. My dear wife to receive some sort of trinket, while the bulk of the estate is to go to a distant relative in Nottingham. The whole business is a sober reminder of mortality, and the futility of greed.

Tuesday, November 9

Yesterday, began in early afternoon sifting through Cracknell's documents and ledgers, Emily having laid a nice fire and lit the lamps, for the weather is uncommon dull at the moment and darkness seems to overtake us at the slightest pretext, and always in complete surprise. I suppose I became utterly absorbed, chasing this, following that, noting the other, turning and reading papers, one after another, and so I was quite shocked to realise in the next instance, when I heard Emily ring the bell downstairs, that it was time for dinner. Afterwards (boiled leg of mutton, caper sauce, parsnips and potatoes) I made my excuses to my dear wife, who seemed somewhat fatigued and who was planning to retire early, anyway, and returned to my task in the study, this time with the added assistance of an invigorating, warming glass brandy.

When Emily next came to enquire if I required anything before she too retired I asked her to fetch the brandy bottle and leave it, and make up the fire, as I intended to work late. She seemed quiet and introspective and I asked her if everything was well, and she said it was. Simply to test her I also said it had been brought to my attention (though I had actually witnessed the event from my study window) that the ostler's boy had been seen loitering outside the house again, but she said she knew nothing of it, fell silent, and then said goodnight.

Worked with great enthusiasm, more or less completing the task of going through all the papers, so that by the time I had decided to end my work the fire had died down, I had drunk a good portion of the brandy and the clock on the mantlepiece said three-eighteen in the morning! Crept off to bed as silently as I could and did not wake until after breakfast. Very rewarding.

Friday, November 12

I have it! I really think I have it. The audacity of the man Crawley challenges my powers of description, but I shall try. I see the matter thus.

Whether or not Crawley was actually an engineer, or what were his origins and his background, do not concern me at the moment. What is significant is that he was in Darlington in 1825 and that he was among the large, excited crowds who stood around the in the vicinity of the Skerne crossing, in sight of Bonomi's fine new bridge, and witnessed if not the actual opening then at least the triumph of the Stockton to Darlington railway. At the same time, whereas many of the witnesses to this historic event evidently poured scorn upon the entire enterprise and treated the spectacle as a huge lark, Crawley seems to have grasped its potential almost immediately. He evidently saw in it something which might change the landscape forever, and in consequence something in which there was money to be made. Whether this was the very first time in his life Crawley seized upon a fraudulent opportunity, or whether this was the first time he thought of it, I do not know. Nor do I know when he dreamed up his little scheme. But the fact remains that, unlike many of the other spectators the spitting kettle machine seems to have planted within him the germ of an idea, and that eighteen months later he had moved to Norfolk, presumably anticipating similar railway expansion in this area.

Somewhere along the way, but possibly in Norfolk (for there is no precise information to the effect that the pair had met earlier), he ingratiated himself with Rennie, somehow talked him into supporting the scheme, and thus provided himself with an ally inside the Holt bank. I would say from that point on, and aside from any terrors relating to possible discovery, Rennie's financial training and his desire for accurate accounting led him to do everything according to the proper procedure. Thus if Crawley withdrew a sum of Porter's money, Rennie duly recorded it. If Crawley dabbled in a landowner's affairs, Rennie quite properly marked the appropriate ledger and accurately noted the information in the correct memorandum. Everything Rennie did he recorded, aside from the nature of the fraud itself, perhaps as a curious means of defence if he was by any chance caught, but also, I think, as a way of not causing alarm. If the books balanced, perhaps, he thought, no one would examine them too closely. In any event it would appear he was not caught, and the bank never suspected anything simply because they did not examine all the accounts and ledgers closely enough.

By now, in the autumn in 1827, Crawley was calling himself a land agent and seems to have been intent on ingratiating himself with the Norfolk land-owning community. If he did work for any of them there is no record of it. More likely he was living on borrowings from the bank supplied by Rennie, perhaps on the grounds that Crawley was busily sowing seed which would bear a harvest later.

It would appear, to judge from dates and signatures among the bank records, that towards the end of 1827 Crawley and Rennie began to put their plan into operation. Their idea - or was it Crawley's idea? - was based entirely on the premise that the railway would become a significant factor in the landscape and that it would spread all over the country. So the plan seems to have been to bankrupt a local landowner, buy his estate lands at a knockdown price, and then sit tight until they could re-sell it at a hugely inflated price to one of the railway companies. To this end the pair began to search for a landowner or farmer, preferably already in financial straits, who owned substantial acreages in an area certain to be attractive to the railway boards.

There is good evidence, gleaned from Rennie's carefully kept and surprisingly modest expenses sheets, that Crawley searched areas around King's Lynn, Cromer and Yarmouth, presumably without success. I believe he also looked at Wells and its surrounding area, which suggests strongly to me that Crawley and Rennie had concluded the railways would serve, first, the areas of most population, and second, the areas of greatest industry, namely, the ports. At some point, however, their efforts narrowed towards Blakeney and ended when, because of Rennie's very useful access to bank records, they came across Mr Aemilius Porter, the possessor of many fine acres stretching in an arc around a large proportion the approaches to the port, and a bank balance of sufficient fragility to send any sensitive wife into a blizzard of fainting fits.

Having once decided upon his course of action Crawley seems to have gone out of his way to introduce himself to Porter, and moreover, evidently managed to persuade Porter to appoint him as his land agent. In certain circles, it would seem, Crawley's ingratiating mannerisms and fawning capabilities were greeted as manna from heaven, even if, according to his journal, they did not fool Hudson. However, knowing Porter was pressed for cash Crawley cleverly offered his services free, drawing up a scheme whereby he would be rewarded if he managed to turn the finances of the farm around. With nothing to lose, at least on the surface, a worried Porter finally agreed and even signed documents to that effect, documents which Rennie later carefully notated and filed among the bank papers.

Crawley's next task was to drain from the farm what remaining capital Porter could muster, and to this end came up with the idea of the drove. He prepared the ground carefully. Scottish runts, he pointed out to Porter - and his calculations are preserved in Cracknell's boxes - were modestly priced in Galloway, whereas St Faith's prices, in 1829, were holding and might even show further increase. If Mr Porter put as much of his capital as he could into the enterprise - in other words, risk everything - the profits would be substantial. They would engage the best drover available, and he, Crawley, would personally travel to Galloway to supervise the purchase of the runts and see the drove on its way.

How long Mr Porter spent mulling over this last desperate proposition is not recorded, but acquiesce he eventually did. Hudson was engaged and financed on the basis that he was the best and most respected drover in the county, and Crawley, also armed with substantial funds, all supplied by Mr Porter, headed north where he rented a large house as a centre for his nefarious enterprise and as a means of impressing Hudson. Almost all of Mr Porter's funds were poured into the enterprise - the bank paper and document work being completed by Rennie - and plans were subsequently made in Scotland not only to lull Hudson into a false sense of security but to actively prevent the drove from reaching Norfolk.

Had the plan worked - in other words, had Hudson's drove not reached St Faiths - there is little doubt that Mr Porter would have been bankrupted. There is little doubt, too, that at that point Rennie would have produced sufficient funds, also from the bank, for the pair to have taken control of the Blakeney acres. But the scheme went awry. Despite losses, most of the herd did get through, thanks to Hudson's fortitude, and it was Hudson, not Porter, who lost everything. Porter survived, just, whereas Hudson was forced to join the ranks of the discredited and poverty-stricken. Crawley and Rennie, their conspiracy uncovered, disappeared from the scene, and there is a certain irony, I suppose, in the fact that the rest of the story really belongs to the innocent but publicly maligned Hudson.

After the drove of 1829, and bereft of wife, reputation, home and belongings, Hudson spent three years in purgatory, living among the lowest of the low, but in 1833 circumstances forced him to return to Holt and there seek charity. To this end he required a settlement from the Justices, and it was this that caused such a stir in the town. When he was refused, only the workhouse remained, and it was towards this that he was preparing to walk when, outside the Shire Hall immediately after the hearing, a lad thrust his way through the throng to hand him a small bag.

I now know the bag contained fifty pounds of bank money, supplied by the manager, Turnbull. The amount was little enough in compensatory terms, but at least it enabled Hudson to live in Holt at a very modest level, a figure of some sympathy until his death a few years later. It is my belief that Turnbull, frightened that Hudson, when faced by the workhouse, might talk publicly of his innocence and Crawley and Rennie's mis-doings, and thus do the reputation of the bank considerable harm, attempted to buy him off, or at least supply him with sufficient money to keep him out of the clutches of parish charity. For whatever reason, and as far as I can tell, Hudson never did talk, neither before the hearing nor afterwards. He kept his own silence, as they say.

The supreme irony is that Crawley's scheme would have failed, anyway. Blakeney never did get its railway, and as far as I can ascertain it probably never will. But Lynn, Wells and Yarmouth did. They flourished, whereas Blakeney's port facilities declined. Of course, all this is my submission, my educated attempt to reconstruct the events of all those years ago; but I believe my modest efforts to be substantially correct.

Saturday, November 27
A most sad and terrible business, which has shocked clergy and congregations throughout the county. It seems that Norwich Cathedral has had to undergo some sort of re-consecration on account of the principal singer committing suicide in the archive room. The corpse was not discovered until documents were required by the Chapter, and someone was sent to collect them. It is such a distressing business, and has caused such widespread dismay, that the Festival of Choirs has been transferred from the cathedral to St Andrew's Hall.

Monday morning
Crisp and bright, and such an inviting day I wrapped well against the cold and strolled for some time around the town, enjoying the bustling vibrancy of the place as it prepares for Christmas. It sometimes occurs to me there is so much to look forward to. A bright new year, a loving family and household, friends and conviviality, holly and bright fires, gaslight and the clatter of hooves and rattle of carriages in the street outside, passersby singing, and swinging lanterns, all casting a homely light upon the snow.

In High Street, opposite the water tower, I stopped and watched an elderly man and two youths drive a flock of turkeys towards the Market Place, and admired the quiet and skilful way in which they maintained their control without ever distressing the birds. Sometimes a passing carriage or a passer-by on the road would cause a small ripple of consternation among the creatures, but each time the drover, or one of his lads, was there to shoo them back into formation, and to calm them, and so they continued, noisily, seemingly without a care in the world. I wondered if the turkeys knew it would soon be Christmas, and if they would change things if they did have this priceless knowledge.

I thought of Brumell, too, who keeps his flock moving in the right direction, and of poor Hudson and of what a clever, determined man he must have been, and it occurred to me then, as I strolled home saying my Good Mornings to my friends and nodding to acquaintances, that although the future can sometimes be changed (though of course it would no longer be the future if it was changed), the past is unavoidable. The past never goes away. It also occurred to me I might be becoming morbid. To counter the possibility, I must remember to think of things which delight me.

Tuesday, December 7
My previous statement is still before me as I write, but I have to record that the week-end was a quite beastly affair, our Christmas shopping expedition to Norwich being quite ruined not only because of the noisiness

of the crowds in that fine city but also because of the weather, namely snow, which made it one of the longest and more tiresome journeys my dear wife and I have ever encountered. Such was the level of snow and the condition of the roadways that our carriage, slipping and sliding nearly the whole of the way, to the great distress of my dear wife, finally became entrapped in the vicinity of Marsham, where there had been much drifting. The groom, stupid fellow, finally tramped off to a nearby stable to hire additional horses, leaving us cold and alone. Naturally, we arrived late at our hotel in Norwich, and with barely time in which to dine, but our misery did not end there. My dear wife decided the rooms were not to her liking, and there was much to-ing and fro-ing, and many discussions, before we were finally able to settle for the night.

We have the Christmas gift shopping done, but there was precious little pleasure in it. My anticipation is quite dissipated.

Friday the 10th
We are to dine shortly at The Feathers with our friends and other important people in the town, there being a projected party of nineteen. My dear wife has gracefully volunteered to take on the onerous duty of deciding upon the constituent dishes of the meal with the man from The Feathers, a task I am confident she will fulfill to the satisfaction and pleasure of everyone.

Monday, December 13
There was a most extraordinary business shortly after midday, as I was at my desk, when there was a sharp knock at my study door and in strode my dear wife, her face set firm and determined. Try as I may I cannot recall the last occasion my dear wife visited my study, she considering it, quite rightly, to be my private preserve. But even the utter surprise at her visit paled into insignificance when set against the news she brought. She glanced around the room, took in the untidiness and chaos, and the piles of papers and documents distributed over every available surface, and finally seated herself somewhat stiffly in my easy chair beside the fire. Then she gathered her thoughts and announced, "Emily has just been to see me. The girl intends to leave our employ early in the New Year in order to marry the ostler's boy."

Shock! Desolation! Oh, agony! Emily to leave us? Oh, desolation!

Recovering my composure, I asked tentatively, "Does she have to marry?"

My dear wife looked at me sharply, confirmed that she too had harboured similar disgraceful thoughts, and replied, "It is my belief she will marry from free choice. In any event she is leaving, and we must endeavour to find a replacement."

The news left me breathless with dismay.

Could she not simply take time off to marry, and then return to us?

No, she could not. There was also the question of her room.

Could she not live elsewhere with her new husband and come in to work every day?

No. That would not serve. She would not be here in the evenings when we needed her, and who would assist with the playing-card parties?

Then the ostler's boy is a villain, and I will not employ him again.

Don't be absurd. I have reason to believe (said my dear wife) that the ostler's lad is a rather fine, upstanding fellow, and Emily will do well by him. Anyway, they are sure to start a family shortly, so in the New Year we must say farewell to her and then find someone new.

Oh! Desolation.

Friday, December 17

An eclipse of the moon visible, which merely increased my deep feelings of melancholy. It would be improper to suggest I face a bleak future if denied the opportunity to see Emily's sweet face each day, but it would be truthful to infer that the girl permanently inhabits a hidden corner of my mind which is unknown to my dear wife.

Sunday, December 19

I have decided, after giving the matter considerable thought, that in the New Year I shall endeavour to place all that I know of the Hudson affair on paper in the form of a vignette. It might prove popular among my circle of friends and even be of interest to some of my acquaintances in the Archaeological Society, though it is my experience, sad to relate, that most of them spend precious little time considering such popular and basic activities as droving, preferring instead to attend dry discussions on the significance of rim decoration on Neolithic funerary pots. But we shall see. I still find the Hudson business, and the time spent thinking about it, a consolation of sorts in the deep well of my depression.

One task which still confronts me is to discover what happened, in later years, to both Crawley and Rennie. The bank man, Rennie, seems to have disappeared completely, and I have seen no further trace of him. Clearly, when the ruse was discovered, or perhaps shortly before, he left the bank, but since then there has been silence. As for Crawley, all I have found among the bank papers is a note written by Turnbull, who was manager at the time, dated February, 1830, describing Crawley as "latterly of Liverpool." But there was no more. Perhaps he still lives there, or died there. Maybe he took ship to the Americas, which many villains seem to have done. I shall try to find out.

Boxing Day
Another Christmas Day over, pleasant enough, but with the jollities somewhat restrained. Our last with Emily, of course, which signals further
changes to come in the little world of our modest household.

Turning cold, with flurries of snow.

Tuesday, December 28
A chain of events was set off today in a most innocuous manner. As is my
usual routine, I was reading the Eastern Daily Press this morning when
my eye was caught by a pair of advertisements on the front page, one
from the Postmaster General advising readers that rates for the new telephone service in the city had been set at £14 10s for subscribers living
within half a mile of the telegraph office, and the other, from the United
Telephone Company, which I believe embraces Bell and Edison interests,
which stated they were the patent holders and that proceedings would be
taken against anyone using Bell or Edison apparatus which had not been
rented from the UTC.

At once, I recalled two matters. One was an incident which occurred
almost thirty years ago, when travelling in the Longham area. I noticed
the cables of some sort of electric telegraph stretching across fields from a
farmer's house to the Parsonage. Upon my inquiry as to the purpose of
the cables, someone in the village said it had been done so that a young
man and a young woman could talk to each other. The matter made me
highly sceptical, and I recall concluding that perhaps they were using some
form of Morse communication, the pulsing system having recently been
invented by Samuel Morse, an American. The advertisements also put me
in mind of the old shutter stations popular at the turn of the century, the
invention of the electric telegraph and, at about the same time as the
Longham business, the introduction of submarine cables to mainland Eu-
rope.

Dear me, I thought, the lengths some people will go to, to avoid having
to write and correspond!

It also put me in mind of a demonstration in the Victoria Hall, Norwich,
by Professor Barrett, perhaps three years ago, which I attended accompa-
nied by one or two friends. The gentleman evidently arrived in the city
with two Bell telephones, one of which was immediately transported to
Cromer and joined to the Post Office line there, in order there might be a
demonstration at the end of the lecture.

The whole matter greatly amused the 40 or so people in the audience.
Prof Barrett spoke of the early experiments of Reis and Gray, Bell and
Edison, using diagrams to explain how the instruments worked, and even

showed us how to make a telephone for a few pence from a tooth-powder box, a small bar magnet, a disc of tinned iron and some wire, all of which was great fun. But when it came to the matter of the actual demonstration, well, nothing happened! Neither Professor Barrett nor Mr JJ Colman, who presided over the meeting and who was uniformly reassuring and courteous, could hear anything more than some indistinct mumbling from Cromer, which they all put down to damage by snow followed by a thaw, and some poorly insulated cable. Anyway, it was great fun, and somewhat late at night we all adjourned to the Maid's Head.

However, when I mentioned the matter to my dear wife this evening, recalling the demonstration in Norwich, and when I pointed out the advertisements in the newspaper - which she does not read because so much news these days is simply too distressing - she became detached and thoughtful, wondering out loud if the telephone would ever become widespread. I told her I thought not. I believe the Great Eastern Railway has trifled with Bell telephones, and J & J Colman have Edison instruments on a telegraph line between Norwich and London, but I did not see how it could possibly be of greater benefit than the written word.

She looked at me and said, "We must hope not."

"Why is that, dearest?"

She said immediately: "Does not the bulk of our income derive from the manufacture of writing paper and envelopes? Would not our financial position be undermined if the telephone did become popular?"

So it would. Naturally, however, I attempted to calm her fears, saying she should leave all matters of commerce and finance to me and that in any event people would never give up corresponding. The telephone would never become popular. But whatever the outcome, be assured my dear wife and I will face the uncertain future with courage and fortitude.

Friday, December 31
New York, I read, has begun to light its streets with electricity, and today there was yet another eclipse, this time of the sun. For a few moments I wondered if the one was eventually destined to eclipse the other, and then decided not. God would not allow the vanity and futile achievement of man to supersede His great works.

All in all it has been a strange year, for there have been many other matters I might have recorded in my commonplace book. I intend to continue these jottings, but there is little doubt much of the news is too sad to be worthy of inclusion. The war news is gloomy, agriculture remains depressed and presumably will continue to be so; Emily is leaving; old age is approaching myself and my dear wife; and now the telephone business, some say, will put an end to writing and thus, in consequence, to our income.

Ah! me. Perhaps Hudson had the balance right after all. He fought to the very end, and with every fibre of his being. In my own way, I too battle to find Salvation. Truly, it is what we all seek. Amen.

And an Epilogue

Norwich, Norfolk
February, 2000

BRIEFLY, NO copies of Mr Hume's 1882 vignette on the Hudson affair - the publication of which was apparently greeted with almost complete indifference by the pamphlet buying public of Holt at the time - are known to survive. Simularly, the sole and original copy of Hudson's own account of the 1829 drove is lost, or at least has not been seen since 1884 when it was listed among a legal inventory of Hume's property completed immediately following his death. It follows, therefore, that had it not been for Mr Hume's commonplace book, which has been granted a temporary place of safety among my shelves, Hudson, the events of the drove, and even Hume himself, would have been completely forgotten.

Life is a fragile enough business, and I am bidden to believe that the past is probably little more than a recurring re-connection with our beginnings. But if that is so, then I am constantly surprised we are so careless with it.

THE END